*Roseanna*

THE SHACKLEFORD LEGACIES
BOOK THREE

BEVERLEY WATTS

BAR PUBLISHING

### Copyright © 2025 BaR Publishing

© 2025 BaR Publishing. All rights reserved. No part of this publication may be reproduced, stored or transmitted in any form or by any means, electronic, mechanical, photocopying, recording, scanning or otherwise without written permission from the publisher.

It is illegal to copy this book, post it to a website, or distribute it by any other means without permission.

This novel is entirely a work of fiction. The names, characters and incidents portrayed in it are the work of the author's imagination. Any resemblance to actual persons, living or dead, events or localities is entirely coincidental.

BaR Publishing has no responsibility for the persistence or accuracy of URL's for external or third party Internet Websites referred to in this publication and does not guarantee that any content on such Websites is, or will remain, accurate or appropriate.

Designations used by companies to distinguish their products are often claimed as trademarks. All brand names and product names used in this book and on its cover are trade names, service marks, trademarks and registered trademarks of their respective owners. The publishers and the book are not associated with any product or vendor mentioned in this book. None of the companies referenced within the book have endorsed the book.

Cover art by wickedsmartdesigns

# One

'I doubt very much that any footman would respond to a request for assistance with quite such a threatening scowl.' Nicholas Sinclair eyed his newest 'member of staff,' with exasperation.

'Perhaps I would react more favourably if the request was delivered in a more agreeable manner.'

Nicholas raised his eyebrows. 'And neither would they respond with such a blatantly inflammatory comment.'

'I thought you wanted his lordship to recruit me. He's not likely to do that if I'm too much the toad eater.'

'He won't do it if he thinks you too much the rabble-rouser either. Brandy?'

Tristan Bernart ran his fingers through his hair in frustration before nodding his head. He muttered, 'I'm not sure I'm cut out to be a servant,' prompted a rueful chuckle.

'I'm bloody sure you're not,' Nicholas sighed, handing over a snifter of brandy.

Tristan took a grateful sip. 'Forgive my dudgeon,' he commented. 'I've waited a long time to expose d'Ansouis, and the whole bloody case rests on my being able to convince the bastard to recruit me.'

'It depends on more than that,' the Duke retorted. 'Recruiting you is just the first step. We have to prove the *Revisionists* are operating under his leadership.'

Tristan Bernart had arrived at Blackmore just before dawn and since that time had been closeted in the Duke's study. So far, the only person outside of the room even aware of the newcomer's arrival was Malcolm Mackenzie – Nicholas's unorthodox valet.

'Roan told me before I left that he should be here before nightfall. When will Fitzroy arrive, your grace?'

'You know, that's the first time you've actually addressed me correctly,' Nicholas answered mildly, sipping his brandy.

Tristan scowled again. 'All this bloody bowing and scraping is enough to set a man's teeth on edge.'

'Nevertheless, bow and scrape you must if we are to catch our man in the act. I know you have more reason than most to hate d'Ansouis, but, if you think you cannot act the part, tell me now.'

Tristan gritted his teeth, then shook his head abruptly. 'I can do it. In truth, I'd bow to the devil himself if it meant bringing the bastard to justice.'

The Duke gave a tight grin before swallowing the rest of his brandy. 'Hopefully, that won't be necessary. In answer to your question, Jamie will be arriving tomorrow. I would like to have you installed by then. Shall we try again?'

~

'How many carriages are we planning to take?' Gabriel Atwood, Viscount Northwood, stared askance at the mountain of luggage in the large entrance hall.

'Darling, we have two daughters of marriageable age who are attending a house party at the country seat of arguably England's most eminent Duke, where there will undoubtedly be numerous suitably appropriate suitors they will need to impress.' His wife Hope's voice rose, and Gabriel winced, putting his hand on her arm to prevent her voice carrying to the furthest reaches of the house. Quiet and softly spoken, his beloved was not.

'There's no need to shout, my love. You have made your point admirably. I am a complete philistine with no grasp of the intricacies of the marriage mart.'

Hope sighed. 'Please don't use that word in front of Roseanna. If she gets a whiff of any potential matchmaking, she'll simply refuse to go. The Lord knows we don't want to give her any excuse to cry off, and as far as her totty-headed notion of allowing true love to find her…' Hope paused and gave a sighing shrug. 'In truth, it's a totty-headed notion they both share.'

'Well, considering that's exactly what happened to us and every one of your sisters, they can be forgiven for harbouring such romantic fantasies.' Gabriel stepped forward and pulled her into his arms. 'I know you are pragmatic above all things, sweetheart, but they're not yet twenty. Allow them their dreams a little longer.' He bent his head and touched her lips with his in the softest of kisses before adding, 'And who knows, both Jenny and Mercy have made love matches, so the Shackleford magic may yet continue.'

Hope willingly sank into her husband's embrace, just as smitten with him now as when she'd first met him as an unkempt vagrant in her father's church almost twenty years ago.

It was true, she and her sisters had all been incredibly fortunate in their choice of husbands, and naturally she hoped her own daughters would have the very same luck. But she was realistic enough to recognise it was unlikely, and while she had no intention of forcing either twin into a union they were unhappy with, neither was she averse to putting things in motion behind the scenes, so to speak. Leaving things entirely to chance was not in Hope's nature, and she firmly believed that sometimes it was necessary to help a happy ending along a bit...

'It will be lovely to see Jennifer again and to finally get to meet Brendon,' Hope mused, eventually stepping out of Gabriel's arms. 'I'm given to understand her father-in-law is making the journey too.'

'Is that the father-in-law who apparently gave Augustus the runaround?' Gabriel asked, suddenly interested.

'The very same,' Hope answered, pulling on her gloves. 'Do we know where Luke is?'

'I sent him to fetch Daniel from the stables. Silas and Henry are going to need assistance in getting the trunks onto the roof of the coach.'

Hope frowned, looking down at the trunks piled up at their feet with fresh eyes. 'Perhaps you should have put some of it in the coach with Gilbert, Doris and Emily,' she commented, referring to the two lady's maids and valet who'd been sent on ahead.

'I did,' answered Gabriel flatly.

With a cringe she hastily covered with a small cough, Hope turned to look up the stairs. 'I think I'd better go and hurry the girls along.'

Gabriel grinned, knowing his wife's tactics of old. 'As you can see, my love, we still have plenty of time. It's going to take an age to load up everything – even with Daniel's help.' He spent a few seconds enjoying the sight of her face becoming mulish before going back to their earlier subject. 'I must say, the prospect of a whole weekend rubbing shoulders with the Mayfair popinjays has suddenly become much more appealing. Do the others know Galbraith the Older is coming?'

'By *others*, I assume you're referring to the other poor unfortunates saddled with a wife whose former name was Shackleford,' Hope retorted. 'And, yes, I assume so, since I received the news in a letter from Grace, and if she had any sense, she'd have simply copied the prose eight times and changed the names.'

Her husband's grin turned into a chuckle. 'Do we know the sawny's name?'

Hope gave a pained sigh. 'Please don't call him that, Gabriel. I'm told he's particularly patriotic and given that there are likely to be several influential members of society present, we really don't want to encourage any north-south of the border rivalry.' She paused and shook her head. 'In all honesty, I think that was the real reason Grace told us all he's coming. She's hoping that members of her family might actually assist in keeping Dougal Galbraith *out* of trouble. Unless we all remain especially vigilant, things are likely to go to hell in a handbasket once he and Father get together.'

~

'Thunder an' turf, girl, what the devil were you thinking of inviting Dougal along?'

'I didn't actually invite him, Father,' Grace responded tartly, ignoring the fact that, though she was nearing fifty, her father had seen fit to refer to her as *girl*. 'It was more of an assumption on Jennifer's part.'

The Reverend snorted. 'You're wrong there. Jennifer would no more have invited that beetle-headed bumpkin than the devil himself.'

Grace finished pouring their afternoon tea. 'I thought you and Mr Galbraith had become friends?' she queried, handing him a cup.

'That doesn't alter the fact that the man's a deuced menace, or the fact that both Jenny and Brendon are fully aware of it. You mark my words, Grace - Dougal has invited himself along.'

He shook his head, helping himself to a biscuit. 'And there can be only one reason for that.' He dipped his biscuit into the tea before sucking on it noisily.

Nibbling on her own biscuit, Grace pondered his words. Naturally, she'd been immediately suspicious when her father invited himself for afternoon tea, but for once it appeared she'd been completely wrong about his motivation. In truth, she'd been expecting him to ask whether she and Nicholas would consider including Percy, Lizzy and Finn on the guest list to Blackmore's annual garden party. Naturally, the small family's invitation was a given.

She bent down to give Flossy the remains of her biscuit before brushing down her skirt. 'So, what do you think his reason is for travelling all the way from Scotland?' she finally quizzed him, wondering if she actually wanted to know.

'Why else would he put himself in the middle of a bunch of Sassenach muttonheads except to cause trouble?' The Reverend shrugged. 'Friends we might be, but Dougal Galbraith will never be a toad eater to the English. I fear he has an ulterior motive.'

Grace frowned. In fact, she had wondered why Brendon's father would wish to accompany his son and daughter-in-law on such a long journey, given that he was no spring chicken.

'Naturally, I'll inform Nicholas,' she said at length, 'and request that someone keep an eye on him. But Jenny and Brendon are already well into their journey. I cannot prevent Dougal accompanying them, even if I wanted to. We can only hope that the rest of the family will have the measure of him by the time the guests begin arriving. And once that happens, I'm certain Nick will nominate someone to watch him.'

The Reverend nodded and helped himself to another biscuit. 'If truth be told, Grace, as much as it pains me to say it, I think that someone has got to be me.'

∼

'How many guests will there be at Blackmore? Are they all staying in the house?' Hope looked at her daughter in concern, well aware that Roseanna's question was not an idle one. She hated being indoors with a crush of people and tended to retreat into her bedchamber whenever they had more than half a dozen guests staying at Northwood. Strangely, she didn't feel quite the same sense of panic when outside.

Though twins, her daughters were not at all alike. While both were possessed of a delightful wit, Francesca was gregarious and outgoing in whatever company she found herself, while Roseanna tended towards anxiety and discomfort whenever she was put in a confined space with lots of people – especially strangers. When quizzed, Rosie said simply that she preferred her own company, or that of her twin.

How on earth she thought true love likely to find her when she spent the majority of her time closeted wherever others were not, her mother had no idea.

Sighing, Hope leaned forward and took Roseanna's hand. 'I dare say there will be more than twenty, but less than fifty. And most of them will be in the East Wing. We will be staying in our usual suite in the West Wing. And the only people staying in the house until Thursday will be family.'

Roseanna squeezed her mother's hand and nodded, giving a small smile. 'Don't worry about me, Mama. I'll be perfectly fine. If the weather holds during the house party weekend, we'll undoubtedly be spending most of the time outside in the gardens. It will be fun. I haven't played croquet in an age.'

'That's because you're dreadful at it,' her brother Luke laughed. 'The last time you played, you flipped the croquet ball up onto Papa's head.'

'I've still got the lump to prove it,' grinned Gabriel.

'In fairness, she had got her heel caught in the sod at the time. It was very muddy, as I recall.' Francesca swallowed her own mirth at the memory as she defended her twin.

Roseanna gave a nonchalant shrug. 'So, I may not have quite the sporting prowess of the rest of you, but I have other skills.'

'*Girls'* stuff,' Luke scoffed.

'Then it's a very good thing I'm a girl,' Roseanna retorted with a smile, reaching over to ruffle her brother's hair.

Luke pulled away with a mock scowl before turning back to his father. 'I know Nick will be there, but did you hear from Aunt Patience? Will Max be with them?' he asked, referring to the two cousins in the family closest to him in age.

'I think everyone with even the slightest Shackleford blood in their veins will be congregating at Blackmore this week,' Gabriel answered drily. 'But that doesn't mean you boys have leave to run riot. There will also be quite a few influential people present during the house party, and Uncle Nicholas will expect you all to be a credit to the family.'

Luke pulled a face, then grinned. 'Don't worry, Papa, we won't let the side down.' He twisted round to look out of the window as his father raised his eyebrows and muttered, 'That's what worries me.'

# Two

Having made the journey to Blackmore many times, Roseanna knew it would take them the best part of a day. Being summer, her father had decided against an overnight stop, but it meant they wouldn't arrive at Blackmore until late evening. To give them all an opportunity to stretch their legs and rest the horses, the Viscount had reserved a private room at an inn near to Honiton. And since Luke had been declaring he was about to faint from hunger, almost from the moment they left the Northwood Estate, they would also be partaking of a light lunch. 'That's if you make it that far,' Francesca had commented darkly on the occasion of his last protest.

The weather was clement enough that they made good time and indeed were pulling into the hostelry by early afternoon. The inn was one they'd stayed at before, and they were swiftly shown into a cosy private room at the rear where a cold repast was ready and waiting. Their coach driver and two grooms stayed with the horses, but the Viscount was assured that both humans and equines would be well looked after.

Naturally, Luke wolfed down his lunch before disappearing outside to the courtyard where he'd seen a couple of lads his age playing

Hopscotch. 'Hopefully, he'll run off a little of his energy,' Hope sighed. 'Otherwise, the next six hours are going to seem like a hundred.'

Fifteen minutes later, Roseanna could no longer suppress her need to use the privy, which was situated at the back of the inn. Since their maids had been sent on ahead, her father insisted all three ladies go together - while the inn was well used and respectable, as always, there was safety in numbers.

Leaving Gabriel to his brandy, the three ladies were shown to the small privy behind the stables. Clearly being the most desperate, Roseanna went first. As she shut the door, she heard Francesca laughingly joke that she'd looked as though she was engaged in a game of hoopla without the hoop.

Afterwards, whilst waiting for her mother and sister to take their turn, Rosie walked towards the sound of yelling coming from the stable courtyard. Standing at the edge, she spied four raggedy-arsed boys crouched over something. Wildly, she cast her eyes round for Luke, but for a few panicked seconds, couldn't see him. Then, abruptly, she spotted him coming out of the stable door, dragging one of their grooms behind him. Her heart gave a thud as she realised he was crying. Thinking the boys might have hurt him, Roseanna picked up her skirts and ran towards them, shouting. Whatever they were doing, they were obviously up to no good. Startled, all four lads fell back, revealing a small bundle curled up unmoving on the cobbles. Seconds later, they scarpered.

Slowing, Roseanna approached the small object cautiously, wondering if it could possibly be a large rat, or even a fox cub. Clearly, whatever it was, it was alive. Looking over at the groom who she knew was about to warn her against doing anything foolish, Rosie shook her head, crouched down, and stared at the bundle. After a few seconds, it lifted its head and incredulously she realised it was a small puppy.

'Where's your mama, little one?' she whispered, hesitantly holding out her hand for the small nose to snuffle.

'They were going to drown it,' sniffed Luke from behind her shoulder. 'They said its mother was dead, and no one wanted it.' Her heart contracting in pity, Rosie knelt without hesitation on the dirty cobbles and reached out towards the shivering body.

'Careful, my lady,' the groom warned, 'it's just a stray, and it could well give you a nasty nip.' But as her fingers stroked the soft head, the dog's small tail began wagging uncertainly and seconds later, it rolled over onto his back, revealing the fact that it was a little girl.

'What on earth are you doing sitting in the dirt, Roseanna?' Her mother's tone was more concerned than angry. Quickly, Rosie scooped the little dog up and held the trembling body close to her chest. Then, climbing awkwardly to her feet, she turned to face her mother and sister.

'It's a dog,' Luke supplied excitedly. 'Those boys were going to kill it.'

'Does it have an owner?' Francesca stepped forward to gently stroke the pup's incongruously sticking-out ears and was rewarded with a tentative lick.

'Be careful,' warned their mother. 'The poor thing undoubtedly has fleas at the very least and quite possibly more maladies besides.'

'It's a stray, I think,' Luke added. 'Those boys said a poacher shot its mother. They were going to drown it. That's why I went to fetch Sam.' He nodded towards the groom.

'It's a girl,' Roseanna clarified, 'and we can't leave her here.'

'Well, what do you suppose we do with her?'

Hope knew full well what the answer would be. All three of her children had been brought up from the cradle on tales of derring-do by their grandfather's foxhound Freddy, who finally died some years ago at the ripe old age of nineteen. And then, of course, there was the exciting story of how their grandfather came upon his next canine companion.

Less than half the size of Freddy, from the day Flossy hurtled into their lives, she shared everything with the foxhound, from his bowl to his basket. What she lacked in breeding, she made up for in sheer pluck.

The little dog had been devastated when her furry hero had died, but the Reverend always told his grandchildren that Flossy carried a bit of Freddy around inside her. How else would a mongrel the size of a large rabbit have a nose equal to that of a foxhound?

Hope sighed, well aware that when they left, the carriage would be carrying an extra passenger.

∽

Tristan laid his meagre bundle of belongings onto the narrow trestle bed and looked around the small bare room he was to share with the two other footmen. Although he was accustomed to sleeping in less than salubrious surroundings, he hadn't had to share those surroundings with others since he'd been taken under Roan Carew's wing. There was barely enough room for the three beds, each with a small bedside table and a wooden chest at the foot. He was well aware it could have been a lot worse. The Duke of Blackmore treated all who worked for him considerably better than others of his class, and many of the current servants were actually sons and daughters of those who'd been serving when Nicholas Sinclair inherited the title.

Sighing, Tristan began to strip off his shirt and breeches. He'd been ordered by the head butler to report straight back to the kitchen as soon as he'd changed into his livery. He'd spent the best part of the day being grilled by the Duke and his valet, Malcolm, but as tired as he was, he suspected his duties were far from over.

∽

'Henrietta and Lilyanna are both here already, according to Mrs Tenner.' Francesca hadn't bothered to knock as she burst into Roseanna's room the next morning. Then she spied the small bundle of fur in her sister's lap. 'I thought Boscastle told you to take her to the stables?'

'I was going to,' Roseanna defended, 'but after I'd fed her, she fell asleep, and I didn't want to wake her.'

'Well, you can't sit here all day,' Frankie declared. 'You've already missed breakfast.' She looked down at the sleeping pup before wrinkling her nose. 'She needs a bath. The bedchamber smells like a sty. What are you going to call her?'

'I think she looks like a Trixie,' Rosie answered, lifting the sleepy dog up to kiss the top of her head. 'Do you think Father will let me keep her?'

Frankie chuckled. 'I think he's already resigned himself to an additional family member. Papa is well versed in which battles to choose.' She plonked herself down on the end of the bed. 'It might be a good idea for you to speak with Uncle Anthony when he and George get here. I'm sure he'll have lots of good advice. I'm certain Nelson was a stray.'

Rosie nodded and climbed to her feet. 'Tell Henri and Lily I'll join you as soon as I've seen to Trixie's bath.'

The two girls headed downstairs, parting ways in the large square entrance hall. Usually tranquil and quiet, Blackmore already echoed with the sound of laughter, giving a good indication that at least a few members of their extended family had already arrived. Francesca nodded and headed towards the small drawing room with its French doors opening out onto the Duchess's private garden.

Clutching the pup to her, Roseanna hurried in the opposite direction, intending to take a little-known family shortcut out to the stables. However, as she turned into the shadowy corridor, she crashed into something solid directly in her path. With a gasped, 'whoomph,' she rebounded and stumbled backwards. For an agonising couple of seconds, she managed to stay upright, until her foot abruptly tangled in her skirts, and she ended up in an ignominious heap on the floor. Fortunately, she managed to hold on to Trixie, who was now sitting in her lap regarding her new mistress in quizzical astonishment - if a doggy expression could ever be described as such.

'Do you always run along dark corridors without watching where you're going?'

The voice was deep and very masculine. It was also quite scathing.

Roseanna's initial mortification gave way to indignation as she stared upwards. Unfortunately, the man's face was lost in the shadows, but his posture was anything but contrite.

'Do you always remain staring at a lady sitting on the floor without so much as an offer of help?'

Her words seemed to jolt the gentleman into action. Muttering something under his breath, he stepped forward and held out his hand. For a second, she did nothing. Then, with a small, annoyed cough, she tucked Trixie under one arm and grasped his proffered hand, allowing him to pull her up from the floor. Once standing, she was able to see his face for the first time. Initially, her eyes were drawn to his riot of black curly hair. That was until her gaze moved down to his eyes. Pure silver, they seemed to stare into her very soul, though his expression indicated he didn't find whatever he saw there to be of particular note. Full lips and an olive-skinned complexion completed the picture. In truth, he was devastatingly handsome. Or would have been without his sneering expression.

Belatedly, she noticed he was also wearing a footman's uniform.

Since her limited interaction with footmen in general hadn't, up to now, included either scornful expressions or contemptuous remarks, her surprise was genuine. Lowering her gaze and stepping backwards, she inclined her head the merest amount and murmured her thanks before attempting to step around him.

Unfortunately, at the very same moment, he sidestepped in the same direction. Startled, her eyes flew back up to his face, only to see his expression had changed from one of disdain to discomfort as he belatedly appeared to recognise his previous rudeness. It didn't sit well on his face at all, and incongruously Roseanna fought a sudden urge to laugh.

He gave a self-conscious cough, muttering, 'Forgive me, my lady. My remarks were both ill-mannered and boorish...' Pausing slightly, he bowed from the waist and added, 'I do hope you haven't sustained an injury.'

Roseanna regarded him in silence for a second, wondering if she should simply sweep past him without deigning to answer. Unfortunately, not only did the width of the passageway preclude any potential sweeping, she didn't think she could carry off a haughty exit if her life depended on it. And since it wasn't in her nature to be discourteous either, she finally offered a polite, 'Think nothing of it,' and gave a hesitant smile. Unaccountably, he drew in a sharp breath, and abruptly she wondered if she was being too forward.

Face flaming, Roseanna clutched Trixie closer. This was precisely the reason she so hated having to converse with strangers, no matter their standing. She found navigating the morass of social propriety not only tedious but, for the most part, completely baffling.

Desperate now to escape, she mumbled a hurried, 'If you'll excuse me,' and waited, staring determinedly at his broad chest. To her relief, he turned aside to let her pass. Had she been aware of his continued scrutiny right up until she turned the corner, she might have been a little more troubled.

# Three

Who the hell was she?

Tristan was well aware he'd acted like a complete scab. Diplomacy had never been one of his strong points. Had he stayed at sea, he suspected he would never have been more than a common seaman. Roan had despaired of him on more than one occasion.

Following in the same direction as the mystery woman, Tris wondered again at her identity. Clearly, she was a member of the family. Then he winced and sighed. Plainly, he hadn't endeared himself to her by his boorish behaviour. At this rate, he'd be out on his ear before the day was out. He thought about her blinding smile. It had taken him completely by surprise. That she was pretty was evident from the start, but there was nothing to elevate her above the usual vapid females he'd grown accustomed to.

Until she smiled. It had hit right in his breeches. How bloody ridiculous was that? His social etiquette might have been a lost cause, but not so his skills in the bedroom – or so he'd been frequently told – and the coin he'd received in thanks spoke the loudest. But for the first time in his life, he fleetingly wondered what it would be like to actually have a proper relationship with a woman beyond the bedchamber...

~

'Well, she looks healthy enough, my lady. No fleas that I can see. She should be smelling a lot sweeter now too. Do you have a collar and lead for her?'

The groom handed over the wet, shivering pup and Rosie quickly wrapped her in an old horse blanket. 'I don't have anything at all,' she confessed.

The elderly groom climbed to his feet and went into the tack room. A few minutes later, he came out with a matching collar and lead. Clearly its previous wearer had been of the lap variety if the large pink bow attached to the collar was anything to go by. 'I reckon one of their graces' guests left it - some years ago, now. I didn't have the heart to throw it away, it being so pretty and all.'

Rosie took it gratefully and, after drying Trixie's coat as best she could, secured the collar around the pup's neck. The little dog immediately began gnawing at the bow under her chin. 'I don't reckon that'll last long,' the groom chuckled.

'Probably not,' Roseanna sighed. Clipping the lead onto the collar, she swivelled the bow around to the back of the dog's neck and got to her feet, giving the lead an experimental tug. Trixie stood her ground, giving her new mistress such a baleful look, Rosie's sigh turned into a rueful laugh. 'I don't think she's got any intention of being a lapdog.'

'Aye. She'll be leading you a merry dance, that one,' the groom agreed, shaking his head. 'Right, I'll be getting on. Let me know if I can be of any more assistance, my lady.'

Rosie gave him a grateful smile and dragged the little dog back out into the sunshine. Truly, Trixie was not impressed with the collar and lead. In the end, Roseanna picked the stubborn madam up and carried her along the path that skirted the kitchen garden towards the sound of voices.

Looking up at the blue sky, Roseanna hoped the weather would hold until the following weekend. She certainly didn't relish being cooped up inside with a bunch of conceited nobs. Then she grinned to herself. She wouldn't dare use that word to anyone other than her twin, though she knew well that both her parents were of the same opinion about England's aristocracy. Indeed, the whole of her family – on the female side at least – were frequently scathing about the *ton*. Mostly because they'd never belonged to the so-called Elite, even though at least half of them had actually married into it. Indeed, she'd first heard the word *nob* from her Aunt Patience, who'd somehow managed to ensnare a marquess - though the how and why of it remained a mystery to the younger members of the family. Rosie only knew it had something to do with the old Queen Charlotte and a diamond.

Not yet quite ready to join her sister and cousins, Rosie, stepped through an archway into the sheltered herb garden. Putting Trixie back down on the ground, she let the little dog sniff around the herb beds, all the while keeping an eye out for Mrs Higgins. Though the cook was well past retirement age, she preferred to spend her twilight years sitting by the fire in Blackmore's kitchen, which she still ruled with a rod of iron. It was the same with Mrs Tenner, the elderly housekeeper. Rosie suspected that both women didn't actually have anywhere else to go. Indeed, most of the Duke and Duchess's retainers had been with the family forever, and any replacements tended to come from the same stock. Boscastle was still called the new butler – even though the old one had been gone for nearly eight years.

Thinking about retainers inevitably directed her thoughts to the uncouth footman she'd bumped into earlier. He was certainly lacking in footman-like tendencies, but there was no denying he was handsome. She wondered if he'd been at Blackmore long. She didn't imagine so. The kind of belligerent attitude he showed towards her would not be tolerated by either the Duke or Duchess. While neither was the least bit condescending, common courtesy was insisted upon at all times – whether above or below stairs.

Fully aware that her idle daydreaming was simply a ploy to avoid joining the noisy gathering she could hear, Rosie wandered through the herb garden for another ten minutes before realising that if she dallied any longer, Francesca would be coming to find her. And her twin would doubtless ring a fine peal over her head.

With a sigh, she picked Trixie back up, and turned towards the distant voices. Before she had the chance to step back through the archway, however, she caught sight of Malcolm Mackenzie hovering next to the tall raspberry canes not ten feet away. She hadn't seen the Duke's valet, or his wife Felicity in an age, and despite her customary reticence, she'd always found the couple excellent company indeed. Smiling, she lifted her arm, just about to reveal her presence, when the object of her earlier musings suddenly appeared around the corner. To her surprise, he walked straight towards the Scot.

Frowning, Rosie dropped her arm. The footman's arrival had dissuaded her from making her presence known, but instead of retreating, she stood still and watched. Feeling Trixie begin to grumble in her arms, she stroked the dog's head gently to quieten her, suddenly convinced that neither man would be happy to know she was observing their meeting.

'Nicholas received word this morning that he's arriving early.' Malcom's voice was low and clipped.

'*Shit*.' Roseanna blinked at the footman's expletive. Malcolm might be a servant in the Sinclair household, but everyone knew the Scot was his grace's friend and confidant. The buffle-head might as well have sworn at the Duke himself.

To her surprise, however, Malcolm just nodded his head in agreement, adding, 'My thoughts exactly.'

'When?'

'The letter states the day after tomorrow. Roan's already here and Nick's hoping Jamie'll arrive late this evening, so at least we'll have a day tae prepare.'

The strange footman ran his hand through his black curls 'It won't be enough. So much is riding on this.'

'Ye dinnae have tae tell me, lad, but a day is all we have. It'll have tae be enough. His grace'll call you to his study first thing in the morning. Ye need tae do something in the meantime that makes it look as though you're in the suds.'

The younger man gave a short, humourless laugh. 'I think I already have. I ran into one of the guests and accidentally knocked her to the ground.' With a thrill, Roseanna realised he was talking about her.

Malcolm raised his eyebrows. 'Who was she, do ye ken?'

The footman shrugged. 'She wasn't long out of the schoolroom. Mousy hair. Fairly ordinary looking until she smiled.' Rosie drew in a sharp, indignant breath.

'Aye, well, she's undoubtedly a member of the family, so I'd keep yer opinions about her looks to yerself laddy. Especially whatever it was ye said tae make the lass smile. If ye see her again, give me a nod. mebbe we can use it as an excuse tae pull ye in tae the study.'

The footman nodded. 'I'd better get back.'

Malcolm gave a brief answering nod before gripping the footman's shoulder and adding, 'Tristan, remember, we dinna want any bloody heroics when the bastard gets here. Ye need tae do just enough to convince him tae recruit ye. *That's all.*' The intensity of the Scot's last words sent a shiver up Roseanna's spine. The younger man gave a fleeting grin and turned on his heel. Seconds later he was gone.

Malcolm remained where he was for a few moments longer, then with a long sigh, and a muttered, 'I'm tae bloody old fer this,' he picked a raspberry, popped it into his mouth and strode towards the house.

*Tristan.* That was his name. Rosie frowned and stepped out through the archway. Her earlier indignation at his less than flattering comments about her had been short-lived. In truth, she was well aware she was no diamond. Thoughtfully, she continued along the path. But, while she might never be all the crack, neither was she entirely bird-witted. Whoever or whatever this Tristan was, he was certainly no deuced footman.

Nicholas's incredulous stare lasted for so long that Grace briefly feared he'd had some kind of apoplexy. But his eventual, growled expletive reassured her that it had only been anger, rendering him momentarily speechless.

Hurriedly, she went to pour him a brandy. 'I know I should have told you before about Dougal,' she apologised, 'but to be honest, it slipped my mind with everything else going on. And when Jenny told me he was coming in her last letter, I simply thought, *what's one more*. And I doubt the Frenchman will be planning any mischief whilst he's under your roof.'

Nicholas took the brandy and sank down into a chair, muttering, 'Let's hope not.' Then he grimaced. 'It's not your fault, my love. I've been so wrapped up in this whole bloody business, I've just left you to get on with all the arrangements. Even if I'd known, there was nothing I could have done. I'm just glad the conversation with your father prompted you to mention it before Galbraith arrived.' He shook his head and took a sip of his brandy.

'How the hell did we get to this, a secret Jacobite loving Scot in the same bloody house as a French rabble-rouser? We'll have to keep them apart, but God knows how the hell we're going to do it.'

'Father said he'd keep an eye on Dougal,' Grace responded, sitting down opposite him.

The Duke sighed, then gave a grim chuckle. 'I never thought the time would come when I'd be grateful for your father's intervention. Do you have any idea when Jenny and Brendon will be arriving?'

'Tomorrow, I think,' Grace answered. 'They sent a rider yesterday to say they'd arrived at Bovey Manor and would be staying for two nights with Anthony and George. I think they're intending to complete the journey together.'

'We can always hope Tony kills him before they get here,' Nicholas sighed.

Grace gave a low chuckle of her own. 'I think any murdering is more likely to be committed by his wife.'

They sat in silence for a few moments. 'It will be hard keeping the secret from the rest of the family,' Grace muttered at length.

Nicholas grimaced. 'Especially Adam. He already suspects something. He knows me too well.'

'Perhaps Jamie will give you leave to share your plans,' Grace speculated.

The Duke shook his head. 'I doubt it. With Roan, that makes four of us involved, excluding you, love. Any more and we risk it getting to the wrong ears. Not that I believe for one moment that any of my brothers-in-law are gossipmongers, but the fewer people who know about the whole havey cavey business, the better.' He climbed to his feet and went to pour himself another brandy. 'It's enough that I'm having to bring this bastard into my home, without risking my family as well.'

'What is Tristan Bernart like? Will he do what's necessary do you think?'

'He's certainly got the incentive, but at the end of the day, he's a pig in a poke.' Nicholas shrugged. 'I do know one thing. He's unlikely to fool anyone for long. He's the least footman-like footman I've ever deuced well come across.'

# Four

Besides Henrietta and Lilyanna, their other cousins Peter and James, were also enjoying the delightful weather under the beautifully decorated gazebo the Duchess had had erected, especially for the occasion.

At four and twenty, Peter was the oldest of the cousins and, as heir apparent to his father, the Duke of Blackmore, he was also the most senior. Next came Lilyanna's older brother, James, who'd just turned twenty. As the oldest son of Temperance and Adam, he was destined to become the next Earl of Ravenstone.

Both Francesca and Roseanna were closest to their cousin, Henrietta, who was only eighteen months younger than they were. Since their mothers were twins, the three of them had been almost inseparable throughout much of their childhood.

The only other person present in the small gathering was Victoria Huxley. Although not a blood relative, she was Anthony's wife, Georgiana's twin sister. She was also the granddaughter of the recently deceased Earl of Ruteledge. At one and twenty, by an unusual quirk of fate, she was in the enviable position of being in charge of her own affairs.

'So, this is the newest member of the Atwood family that Frankie's been telling us about,' James smiled, climbing to his feet as Roseanna approached the gazebo.

After bending his head in welcome, he wasted no time crouching down to say hello to Trixie, who was more than happy to play to the crowd as she rolled over onto her back.

'I have to say she's a little peculiar looking,' Henrietta declared in her usual forthright manner. 'Her ears stick out at right angles.' Then she gave a rueful grin before adding, 'Much like mine really.'

'Your ears don't stick out, Henri,' Lilyanna retorted. 'Well, not much anyway. And your hair covers them admirably.'

'Unfortunately, none of us have been quite blessed with your looks, Lily,' Francesca declared with a sigh.

'Just be grateful you haven't got her temperament,' James snorted.

'Thank you, brother dearest,' Lily responded with a saccharine sweet smile that promised retribution later. 'I happen to be very happy that I take after my mother.' She stopped at the sudden peals of laughter. 'What?' she added crossly.

'Well, given that Aunt Tempy's *temper* tantrums are legendary,' Peter chuckled, 'my sympathies definitely lie with James.'

Lily stuck out her tongue before turning her back on the two men. 'Have you heard from George, Tory?' she asked Victoria.

After a quick glance towards Peter, which none of the female cousins missed, Victoria gave a diffident smile. 'She was perfectly well when I left, as was little Henry. He's walking now - I don't know who's giving Anthony the most trouble between the two of them. I think they're waiting for Jenny and Brendon to arrive before coming down to Blackmore together.'

'Have Aunt Chastity and Uncle Christian arrived yet?' Rosie asked, sitting down in James's vacated seat and lifting Trixie onto her lap.

'You'd know if they had,' Peter scoffed. 'Olivia and Kate would already be causing mayhem. I feel so sorry for Kit.'

'What about Aunt Charity and Uncle Jago?'

'They've been staying at Cottesmore,' Henrietta informed them. 'I think Uncle Jago has been helping Nate with the renovations to Carlingford Hall.'

'I assume that means they'll all be arriving together en masse, then.' James winced. 'Poor Kit. I hope he gets to travel in Aunt Charity's carriage with Arthur and Tris.'

'I'd say poor Nate,' retorted Peter. 'There's no doubt he and Mercy will get burdened with Elowan, Olivia, and Kate for the journey. The twins are Mercy's shadows when she's with them and I doubt Elowan will want to miss out.'

'I'm looking forward to seeing Jenny and Mercy again,' Victoria confessed. 'It seems an age since the three of us were together.'

'And now, they're old married women,' laughed Lily.

'It's so long since we've *all* been together,' Francesca added. 'I do wonder if Uncle Nicholas is regretting it yet.'

'Oh, assuredly,' Peter declared cheerfully. 'And we haven't even mentioned Aunt Patience and Aunt Prudence yet. I predict fun times ahead before we all have to mind our p's and q's when the important guests start arriving.'

'Is Max coming?' Roseanna asked. 'Luke will be devastated if he doesn't.'

'I'm not sure, to be fair,' Peter shrugged. 'He hates gatherings like this more than you do, Rosie.'

'I do not,' Roseanna's response was a little too indignant.

'Me thinks the lady doth protest too much,' laughed James. Roseanna pulled a face at him, just as the subject of their conversation walked out through the French doors.

'Max!' The chorus was so loud, the future Marquess of Guildford stopped dead in his tracks with a wince.

'I was looking for Luke and Nick,' he mumbled.

'Lovely to see you too cousin,' Peter grinned. 'I think your partners in crime are currently down by the lake with Josh and Emma.'

With a nod and a shy smile, Max turned and hurried back inside.

'So, do we know when Aunt Prudence and Uncle Jamie are due to arrive?'

'Tonight,' Rose answered without thinking. Then her face flamed at the enquiring looks and she stammered, 'I overheard Malcolm telling one of the footmen.'

'I didn't know you'd already seen Malcolm.' Francesca frowned. 'Was Felicity with him?'

Roseanna heartily wished she'd kept her mouth closed. Her face was now the colour of a ripe tomato, and worse, she could tell that her cousins were almost certainly suspecting there was a little more to the story than she was letting on.

She gave a small, self-conscious cough. 'Err, no she wasn't, and err... Malcolm didn't see me, I just happened to be passing...' She stumbled to a halt.

Fortunately, Mrs Tenner chose that moment to appear with three maids in tow, all carrying trays of lemonade. As the drinks and Mrs Higgins' homemade shortbread were passed around, the discussion was forgotten by everyone apart from Rosie.

She'd instinctively chosen not to share what she'd overheard – but only partly because she was embarrassed to admit she'd been eavesdropping. In truth, the main reason was the worry she'd clearly seen in the normally unruffled Scot's eyes.

Dinner that evening was a predictably lively affair. The members of the family that had already arrived congregated in the small, informal dining room, with even the younger children taking their meal with the adults and older siblings. This would continue until the rest of the guests began arriving, at which time the evening dinner would be switched to the large, formal dining room and the younger cousins relegated to the nursery for their evening meal. As she took her seat, Rosie wondered where her grandfather was. In her experience, he never missed out on a free meal, but then she supposed he wouldn't usually have to share it with quite so many.

To her consternation, however, Tristan, *whatever-his-name-was*, was one of the footmen waiting on the table. Though, on this occasion, his behaviour was impeccable. There was no sign of any belligerence at all, and he smiled and bowed graciously as he delivered the food and collected the plates. If he was still planning to make a cake of himself, as Malcolm had suggested, he was running out of time to do it during dinner. Perhaps he believed their earlier collision would be enough. Her mind abruptly conjured up a picture of their encounter in the passageway and the odd look in his eyes as she'd smiled. For some reason, the memory of that look did strange things to her stomach.

Although she tried hard to hide it, there was no denying that her eyes strayed to the handsome retainer far too much during dinner. He, on the other hand, did not look at her once. She told herself she was relieved, but when she caught him smiling at Lilyanna, she felt an entirely unexpected annoyance. What the deuce was wrong with her, for goodness' sake?

Gritting her teeth, Rosie stared down at her plate, her usual robust appetite completely gone. A sudden commotion at the other end of the table had her lifting her head in time to see Tristan inadvertently tip a dish of custard into the Duchess's lap. Here, obviously, was the indiscretion that would get him supposedly hauled over the coals on the morrow.

Roseanna watched Grace carefully as she rose to her feet, waving away the footman's apologies and holding her skirt up to prevent the liquid seeping onto the floor. Abruptly, Rosie realised that her aunt had been waiting for the blunder. Whatever was going on, the Duchess was aware of it too.

As Grace walked swiftly down the length of the table, naturally, everyone's attention was drawn to her. Rosie, however, kept her focus on Nicholas. Even so, she caught very little of his low-voiced reprimand - aside from a time. Eleven a.m. Evidently, that was when the miscreant would be reporting to the Duke's study.

By the time the Duchess reappeared twenty minutes later, the dessert course had been cleared away and her grace smoothly suggested that the ladies retire to the drawing room, leaving the men to their port.

As Roseanna trailed behind, she looked around to see if there was somewhere she might loiter to listen to the gentlemen's conversation. Then she recalled that Malcolm had mentioned her Uncle Jamie. He and Aunt Pru had not yet arrived, and she doubted the Duke would discuss something that was clearly sensitive without the magistrate's presence.

Of course, she knew fully that it wasn't polite to eavesdrop, but her curiosity had been piqued, and wrong or no, she intended to do her utmost to listen in to the conversation taking place in the Duke's study the next morning...

∽

Under normal circumstances, Augustus Shackleford would actually be contemplating Dougal Galbraith's visit to Blackmore with a little more enthusiasm, even though they'd only parted a matter of months ago. However, on this occasion, the very idea was playing havoc with his gout and giving him sleepless nights.

It wasn't just the thought of the potential trouble Dougal could cause - ordinarily he'd be relishing the thought of keeping the temperamental Scot out of mischief. The Reverend wasn't exactly sure what had changed, or when. Indeed, he spent the better part of an hour in the Red Lion as he waited for Percy to finish Evensong, contemplating just that.

Eventually, just as the curate appeared at the door, the Reverend finally concluded that the difference on this particular occasion was Finn. The thought of the irascible Scot leading the lad astray filled him with a sense of foreboding he'd never before experienced – not throughout three marriages, nine children and twenty-three grandchildren. Why that should be so, the clergyman had absolutely no idea, but he had to assume that the Almighty had something to do with it.

As Percy came over to the table with two tankards of ale, Reverend Shackleford couldn't decide whether to share the news of Dougal's impending visit, or simply fudge it. But since he couldn't shake the belief that his Heavenly Master had taken an interest in Finn's welfare for an important reason, the Reverend knew that telling a bit of a plumper wasn't an option. Unfortunately, pitching the gammon wasn't the only option that was inexplicably no longer available to him. For some reason, he felt an unexpected reluctance to share his concerns about Dougal's questionable morals with his curate.

Unfortunately, Percy clearly didn't appear to have the same presentiment of doom at the thought of Dougal's visit. Indeed, the curate was quite enthusiastic, declaring how much he was looking forward to making Mr Galbraith's acquaintance. 'Any friend of yours, Sir, is a friend of mine,' he enthused. 'It'll be nice for the lad to see someone from Caerlaverock.'

Stalling for time, Augustus Shackleford took a sip of his ale, while his mind tried in vain to devise a foolproof plan to avoid just that. After five whole minutes, he'd only managed to come up with one idea, but unfortunately, he didn't think fabricating an outbreak of smallpox up at the house would be on the Almighty's list of approved options.

That was when Percy added, 'Perhaps Mr Galbraith would like to come for dinner.'

~

As the younger children were finally taken up to bed, Roseanna too excused herself on the pretext of taking Trixie out for a brief turn in the garden before bed. She was aware of her mother's anxious look, but on this occasion, it wasn't simply an excuse to disappear. In fact, Rosie had enjoyed her extended family's company. But it was a lovely evening, still light outside, and she felt that Trixie had been left for long enough.

That said, although the evening had been surprisingly agreeable, she breathed a sigh of relief that the game of charades they were all playing as she slipped away meant that no one offered to accompany her.

Five minutes later, she was attaching the lead to Trixie's collar - already minus the pink bow, which was now a scrap of satin on the bed. The little dog was ecstatic to see her and spent the next couple of minutes dashing excitedly backwards and forwards to the door while Rosie threw on her shawl.

Taking the now familiar route to the kitchen garden, and then on towards the less formal areas, Roseanna didn't yet dare let her new furry companion off the lead, since the grass was dotted with rabbits all coming out to feed in the dusk. Idly, she wondered how Mrs Higgins prevented the rascals from eating all her greens. She hoped they didn't resort to traps.

Enjoying the deepening twilight, she wasn't paying attention to where she was going - which was when she discovered that Rabbits weren't the only obstacles to avoid in the greensward. It appeared that a number of moles too were enjoying Blackmore's lush bounty. In the dusk, she didn't see the small pile of soil and inadvertently stepped directly into a mole hole.

Fortunately, the perpetrator was not in said hole as her foot plunged down, so didn't end up flattened. However, that was the only good thing about the sorry situation. As she went down with an unladylike, 'Woomph,' for the second time that day, Rosie abruptly found herself sprawled backwards, her skirts round her knees, scandalously revealing her petticoats. Dazed for a full second, she didn't immediately register the deep, vexingly familiar male voice.

'I must say, my lady, that you appear to have a singular talent for tripping over your own feet. Perhaps you should consider keeping to more well-lighted areas.'

Lifting her head, Rosie stared in incredulous dismay at Tristan, the almost footman, standing not two feet away. As her disbelieving eyes travelled down from his face to his feet, thence onto her own bare legs, she uttered a small, mortified groan and struggled into a sitting position.

'What are you doing, sneaking about in the dark?' she demanded, frantically pulling at her skirts to cover her legs. 'Are you following me?' The question came out far more shrilly than she'd intended, and for one awful second, she had to fight the urge to burst into tears.

Fortunately, she still had hold of Trixie's lead, and the little dog didn't appear to have suffered any ill effects from her mistress's second unexpected contact with the ground in less than twenty-four hours. Without looking up at her tormentor, she swapped the lead into her other hand and endeavoured to lift her foot out of the hole.

Unfortunately, that was easier said than done. Despite tugging, her foot remained firmly wedged. 'Damnation,' she muttered under her breath, hardly listening to his assertion that he was neither sneaking nor following her but had been asked by the Duke to attend the main gates in readiness for the arrival of Mr and Mrs Fitzroy.

'Pru and Jamie have arrived?' she asked, pausing her tugging and looking up at him.

'I believe they are expected presently,' he returned shortly, staring down at her in what could only be described as amused exasperation. Roseanna narrowed her eyes. *Was the arrogant coxcomb laughing at her?*

'I might well be a trifle clumsy on occasion,' she snapped, 'but clearly your manners remain as woeful as ever. Mayhap I shall inform his grace of your ungentlemanly conduct. That will give him another excuse to drag you into his study on the morrow.'

He stared down at her without answering, and a second later she realised what she'd said and could have bitten out her tongue. It was obvious he was wondering at her use of the word *excuse*. Gritting her teeth, she broke their eye contact and resumed her efforts to draw her foot out of the hole.

After another moment, he sighed and stepped forward. 'Give me your hand … my lady.' She didn't immediately look back up. His pause before using her correct address seemed somehow deliberate. She knew nothing about this man, but even so, a goodly portion of her suspected he was actually enjoying her discomfiture.

Glaring up at him, she pursed her lips and held up her hand. For some reason, the feel of his large, warm fingers surrounding hers felt ridiculously intimate, and she was glad that the encroaching darkness hid her blush. His pull was surprisingly gentle as he instructed her to be careful as she eased out her foot. Seconds later, she was standing beside him, and he abruptly let go of her hand as though scalded.

'Does it hurt?' he asked gruffly, stepping away from her.

Roseanna rotated her foot experimentally and shook her head. 'I think it's bruised, but nothing more,' she declared with relief.

'And you're able to walk on it?' he continued. The huskiness had disappeared, replaced by polite but distant concern. At her nod, he gave a slight bow, 'Then, if it pleases you, my lady, I'll bid you good night and continue on my errand.' She nodded, equally frostily, in return, then watched as he strode off into the gathering darkness, remaining still until his retreating figure finally disappeared into the gloom.

Of all the people to witness her foolishness, it would have to be him. 'Conceited muttonhead,' she muttered crossly. Feeling a little better, she looked down at Trixie, who was now busy rooting around the mound of soil surrounding the hole she'd stumbled into. Then, gathering the little dog's lead, she headed as quickly as her sore ankle would allow back towards the house before the light was lost entirely.

# Five

Tristan sighed as he made his way toward Blackmore's gatehouse. Of all the bad luck running into the same bloody woman – but at least her tumble had nothing to do with him this time. In truth, coming upon her as he did – just as she stepped blindly into the hole -- he couldn't have left her to her own devices. She was deuced lucky she didn't break an ankle.

Unfortunately, rather than the danger she was in, his thoughts were, even now, occupied by the sight of her slender legs uncovered as she fell backwards. He'd actually been able to see the tops of her stockings. He gritted his teeth. It was ridiculous that even picturing it caused the kind of stirring he'd last felt as a green boy.

And when he'd taken hold of her hand… He shook his head, quickening his pace. This kind of complication was the last thing he needed. He hadn't had a prigging since he'd left London, that was all. He gritted his teeth - if all went to plan, he wouldn't be getting one in the near future either, so he needed to put any carnal thoughts about slender ankles and dazzling smiles firmly aside and get on with the bloody job at hand. Then his steps faltered as he thought back to her use of the word *excuse*. It seemed a strange term to use, and he found himself wondering if she somehow knew of their plans. Then he shook his head again and shrugged. How the devil would she know anything? She was simply an empty-headed chit with no thoughts between her ears aside from her next ball.

And if a small voice inside his head argued that she hadn't seemed that way at all during their two encounters, he resolutely ignored it.

∼

Nicholas stared in disbelief at the letter in his hand - the one he'd been handed by Boscastle not five minutes earlier. The news it contained was nothing short of catastrophic. Unfortunately, he'd already sent Tristan down to meet with Jamie and Prudence, but his brother-in-law would have to be informed. In a rare fit of anger, Nicholas screwed the paper into a ball and threw it towards the wall. He was getting too bloody old for this. Seconds later, he grimaced, and climbing to his feet, went over to pick it up. His back gave an ominous crack as he bent down, and his ire was replaced by a dry chuckle. Smoothing the sheet out, he looked again at the missive. The news would have to be broken to two brothers-in-law before Roan and Jamie sought their beds, so at least he wouldn't be the only one getting very little sleep this night. Malcolm too would have to postpone any thoughts of slumber. Grace had already retired, and Nicholas decided against disturbing her. She at least could wait until the morning without this additional nightmare to intrude on her dreams.

And he needed to send a missive to Anthony so at least he could inform Jennifer and Brendon of the delicate situation they'd found themselves in.

But there was one other person he'd have to apprise in advance -and just the thought of it was enough to give him an apoplexy. With another sigh, he climbed to his feet and went to his desk, pulling a sheet of paper towards him and taking up his quill...

∼

Roseanna was up early the next morning, more determined than ever to find out exactly what the Duke and Duchess were involved in. Why it should be so important to her? She chose not to question. She wasn't particularly inquisitive by nature, but then she'd never come across a footman who wasn't really a footman before.

Well, in all honesty, that wasn't quite true. Her Uncle Nicholas had several retainers specifically used by members of the family as protection during long, possibly hazardous journeys. As far as she remembered, they masqueraded as anything from grooms to footmen whenever called upon. Could this Tristan be one of those?

It was possible, she supposed. But somehow, she didn't think so. Most servants possessed a natural air of subservience, whereas everything about Tristan, *whatever his name was,* suggested he thought himself equal. But if he wasn't an actual servant, what was he? And what havey-cavey business could he be involved in with her uncle? Malcolm spoke about him being recruited by someone. Did he mean Tristan to infiltrate some nefarious plot?

She'd heard tell that the Duke of Blackmore had been called upon to assist the Crown on several occasions and was even involved in preventing an assassination attempt at the old King George IV's coronation. Though she didn't really know much about it, she did know that the plot had also involved Uncle Jamie who'd been a Bow Street Runner at the time. Sooo... putting two and two together – could this be something of that ilk? Something involving treason towards the new king?

Rosie felt a sudden thrill of fear as she thought about the possibility of someone again targeting the Crown. King William IV had been on the throne for barely a year. While politics were not something she generally thought about, she was aware of talk about a possible reform bill –she didn't know exactly what it entailed – only that her mother and father had spoken about it. How or why proposals for reform might lead to someone wanting to assassinate the King, she had no idea. She grimaced. It all seemed terribly far-fetched.

She knew well that she could very well end up in over her head by trying to discover what was going on. But for some reason, she felt an urge to pursue it - however foolish. Sighing, she climbed out of bed and parted the curtains. It was still early, not long past dawn. The maid wouldn't be in for another hour at least. Shrugging off her nightgown, she pulled on the only day dress she possessed that didn't have hundreds of buttons down the back. Then, throwing a shawl over her shoulders to cover any fastenings she may have missed, she cautiously opened the door to her bedchamber.

While Trixie looked at her enquiringly, the little dog made no move to jump off the bed, and as Roseanna put her fingers to her lips, her furry companion dropped her head back onto her paws and closed her eyes.

A couple of minutes later, Rosie was tiptoeing down the main staircase. If she remembered correctly, the Duke's study was close to the library. On reaching the large square hall, she strode quietly but confidently towards her destination. If anyone asked what she was doing abroad so early, she could say she was looking for a book to read.

Happily, she saw no one, and in no time at all, she was slipping through the door into Blackmore's impressive library. Once inside, she couldn't help but stop and stare. It was a couple of years since she'd last spent any time in the opulent room, and she'd forgotten quite how magnificent it was.

After a few moments, she remembered why she was there and turned left towards the wall dividing the study and the library. The room was quite dark with muslin covering most of the large picture windows - no doubt to protect the books, and she had to tread carefully to avoid crashing into large pieces of furniture in the dimness. On reaching the wall, she stood for a second, looking for a portion that wasn't covered in bookshelves. There would be no chance of overhearing anything with shelves and books in between the two rooms.

Rosie was just about to give up when she spied a small, narrow door incongruously situated at the very end of the shelves. She'd missed it at first, as it was partly obscured by the window drapes. Her heart beating ridiculously fast, she hurried to the door. She guessed it had to lead into her uncle's study. She tried lifting the latch, but predictably it was locked. Pursing her lips, she looked behind her before laying her head against the wood. There was no telling whether she'd be able to hear anything through it, but she'd read that if one had a glass, it would amplify whatever was being said. If she was careful to cover herself with the drapes, she wouldn't be spotted by anyone else using the library.

Her mind made up. She was anxious to get back to her bedchamber and was just about to turn away when she heard the sound of voices coming from the other side of the door. In sudden excitement, she put her ear against it.

'There has to be one here somewhere. Sinclair wouldn't keep the bloody thing anywhere else.'

'He's hardly going to leave something like that lying around for anyone to pick up. At the very least, it's going to be under lock and key.'

Roseanna didn't recognise either voice. While they were reasonably cultured, they didn't have the refined, nasally tones that traditionally characterised members of the upper-class.

'You try the desk, and I'll go through the cupboards. We might get lucky, and at least we can tell his nibs we tried. Remember to leave everything exactly as it was. The last thing we want is for Sinclair to know that someone's been nosing in his private bloody sanctum.'

Rosie's heart was beating almost too loud for her to hear what was being said. She swallowed, endeavouring to calm herself down. Was there time for her to fetch her uncle? Or even Malcolm? But she couldn't guarantee that either of them would be in their bedchambers. By the time she'd tracked them down and explained that someone was illicitly searching the study, the miscreants would likely be long gone. Better for her to remain where she was and find out as much as she could.

The two voices went quiet for the next few minutes, apart from the occasional muttered epithet. Whatever it was they were looking for, they didn't appear to be having much luck. From what she'd overheard, they clearly didn't want to risk leaving any trace of their presence.

As the minutes ticked by, she could hear their movements becoming more frantic. Evidently, they were getting desperate. The longer they were there, the more likely they were to be found. A sudden thought occurred to her. If she headed back into the corridor now, she might be able to catch sight of the perpetrators as they left the study. The thought of possibly coming under the varmint's scrutiny filled her with terror, but if worse came to worst, she could just act as though she was simply passing. She nibbled at her fingernails in indecision. What was beyond the library? The noises next door continued, but she knew she had only seconds to decide what to do. In the end, the heated words she overheard next made the decision for her.

'We daren't stay here any longer. The maid'll be in any minute to set the fire. His nibs'll just have to get hold of another copy somehow. At the end of the day, as long as the bastard's dead...'

A sudden stab of fear rooted Roseanna to the spot. Did they plan to assassinate her uncle? Could it be that these men weren't just thieves, but murderers? What if they came into the library next? Her instinct was to run. But if they did come in, she might well bump into them on her way out. She bit her lip to stifle a frightened moan and stepped closer to the window, wrapping herself in the muslin drapes.

There she stood, hardly daring to move, her whole being focussed on the movements next door. She could still hear voices, but it sounded as though they'd given up the search and were now making sure they'd covered their tracks. A moment later, to her overwhelming relief, she heard the study door open and close, followed by blessed silence.

*~*

*'The thing is Agnes, I'm going to need your help.'* Augustus Shackleford could never in a million years have envisaged himself actually saying those words. Even practising them in front of a mirror brought him out in a cold sweat. He really needed Percy. But the Almighty had put a kibosh on that.

He gave a sigh. Perhaps some fresh air would do him good. It was still early, but at least he'd be assured of some peace and quiet. Calling to Flossy, he made his way downstairs and through the still silent kitchen.

Once outside, he took a deep breath. He couldn't deny that this sudden attack of conscience, the Almighty had seen fit to saddle him with, had really put him in the basket since it meant he couldn't confide in Percy as was his usual wont - for fear of casting aspersions on Dougal Galbraith. So, somehow, he'd have to keep the troublemaker away from Finn without alerting Percy as to why. In truth, the Reverend never really had a problem calling a spade a spade in the past, and while he might have been a trifle blunt on occasion, things had usually sorted themselves out before too much harm was done. Evidently, the Almighty wasn't of the same opinion. The Reverend could even see His point, but tare an' hounds, this sudden advent of noble-mindedness *now* was deuced inconvenient. And it certainly made his upcoming task all the more difficult.

In fact, doubly so, since he'd discovered the missive from Nicholas waiting for him when he returned from the Red Lion late last eve. Indeed, the news therein put his concern about wrongly defaming his Scottish friend at the back of the queue, since there was another, potentially more explosive reason that Reverend Shackleford would need to keep the Scot out of mischief.

In the letter, Nicholas revealed that the former Prime Minister – Arthur Wellesley, the First Duke of Wellington, and the current Prime Minister – Charles Grey, the Second Earl Grey, would *both* be attending the garden party at Blackmore. It was therefore imperative that Dougal Galbraith be kept on as short a leash as possible. Reverend Shackleford groaned. Thunder an' turf, this was getting more complicated by the minute. Indeed, given this new, perturbing news, his best option would have been to share the responsibility for the troublesome Scot with Percy, Lizzy and Finn.

Augustus Shackleford sat down on the wall and desolately put his head in his hands. It wasn't often he was entirely bereft of ideas. Sensing his misery, Flossy put her front paws onto his lap and licked his nose. Shaking his head, the Reverend stroked her soft head. 'We're in the deuced suds and no mistake, Floss. I know the Almighty's got a peculiar sense of humour on occasion, but this time he's outdone himself. I daren't leave old Dougal and Finn together, but I can't tell Percy the why of it.'

In truth, his entire issue lay with the fact that he simply wasn't accustomed to dealing with such a thorny problem without his curate's assistance. He thought again about the possibility of asking for his wife's help. But how the devil could he allow Agnes within a full mile of two of the most powerful men in England? He wouldn't put it past her to accidentally poison one of them.

So, who did that leave? Who could he get to help him ensure that Dougal did not inadvertently (or otherwise) set relations between England and Scotland back over eighty years and potentially cause another Culloden?

# Six

By the time Rosie arrived back in the safety of her bedchamber, her fear had subsided, and she was berating herself for not trying hard enough to discover the identity of the two men. Since she was far too fired up to climb back into bed, she decided to take Trixie outside to do her business. There was always the chance that she would hear and recognise the scoundrels' voices – though she acknowledged it unlikely. After all, she'd heard them through a door.

As she carried a reluctant Trixie outside, she thought about how she was going to enlighten the Duke about the invasion of his study. Though she'd known her Uncle Nicholas for the whole of her life, she didn't really *know* him, and Rosie couldn't deny she'd always found him a little intimidating.

As the highest-ranking member, he was deferred to by the whole family, though it wasn't simply because of his title. Mayhap it was in part because his wife was the eldest sister and he and Grace had married first, but more than that, he'd always taken the welfare of his wife's extended family very much to heart – believing unreservedly that they were all his responsibility. Naturally, as more of the sisters married, his duties became less onerous - indeed, his closest friends were his brothers-in-law, which, of course, could be partly because of gratitude...

However, while he'd always been the person everyone went to whenever there was a problem, Roseanna couldn't help being apprehensive at the thought of coming to the stern man's attention- especially as the knowledge she wished to share with him had come about through prying into affairs that were essentially none of her business.

Still, there was nothing she could do about that. She'd simply have to take the set down with good grace. But when best to do it?

She fleetingly thought of confiding in her father, but since she didn't know whether her uncle had shared the whole smoky business with anyone other than the four people she knew about, doing so might well cause more harm than good. No, she needed to speak to the Duke. And in a place she would be sure to get his attention.

As she walked along the path, Rosie kept an eye out for anyone looking particularly shady, but as it was, she saw no one at all and consequently was able to spend the time deliberating on how best to approach her uncle. Finally, after doing a full loop of the house, she reluctantly concluded that the only time she could be sure of his undivided attention would be while he was in his study. And, while she wasn't privy to his schedule for the day, she could be certain he'd be in there at just after eleven o'clock this morning. He'd have to listen to her then...

∽

Despairing he might have been, but the Reverend's character was basically that of an optimist. By the time he and Flossy had done a full circuit of Blackmore village and returned for breakfast, he had at least an inkling of a plan, though on this occasion it was an unusually simple one. Broadly speaking, it entailed depositing the whole deuced problem at his son-in-law's door.

Augustus Shackleford decided he was simply far too old to tackle a dilemma such as this and, after all, it wasn't his fault his granddaughter had decided to bring her meddlesome father-in-law along. All he needed was for Nicholas to nominate someone to assist him in keeping Dougal Galbraith occupied and out of mischief until the garden party was over. Obviously, it would have to be someone who wouldn't be too unhappy at the thought of missing out on all the hobnobbing – though the Reverend would rather have Flossy chew his toenails off than spend time consorting with politicians and peacocks, so that part of the whole deuced business didn't concern him at all.

According to Grace, Dougal would be arriving tomorrow, and the Reverend knew acutely that he needed to have his strategy entirely in place before the Scot had time to do any damage. Though Nicholas hadn't yet informed him when the Duke of Wellington and Earl Grey would arrive, he knew it wouldn't be until Thursday at the earliest. Until then, there would only be the family at Blackmore. But that didn't mean Dougal could be left to his own devices.

While he was eating his porridge, Reverend Shackleford made notes. It wasn't something he normally did as he generally relied on Percy to do all the tedious bits - he'd always hated dealing with trifles. However, experience told him that when the Almighty stepped in, too much complaining would simply see him burdened with an additional problem that would very likely be worse. So, at the end of the day, it was better to just get on with it. Though looking at his scribbles, the Reverend wasn't entirely sure he'd be able to read them should he ever have need. Hopefully, whoever Nicholas delegated to assist him would also have a good pen.

By the time he put the last mouthful of porridge on the floor for Flossy, Augustus Shackleford concluded that there was no time to lose. He looked down at his pocket watch. If he set off now, he should arrive at Blackmore just after eleven o'clock...

## March 1808

The boy huddled in the corner of the pitch-black cell. With no blanket and no food in his belly, he would almost have welcomed death. Almost.

He'd lost count of the number of days he'd been here. One day merged into another, though he had a suspicion he'd been lying on the stone floor for a long time. On the rare occasions the sun shone through the tiny grill set high in the stone wall, it seemed to have moved.

But he didn't know if it was winter or summer. The temperature never seemed to be anything other than freezing. But if it was summer, then surely, he wouldn't feel this cold right down into his bones as though he was about to turn into one of the ice sculptures the monks used to make before Mont Saint Michel became a prison.

Sometimes he fancied he could still taste the apple that had led to his downfall. The judge had said he'd been tempted by the serpent, like in Adam and Eve. The boy just wished the devil had seen fit to tempt him with a block of cheese. And in truth, he was certain he'd have sold his soul willingly if the exchange had been a hot meal.

Before he'd been thrown here, he'd never imagined prison would be such a quiet place. Broken only by of the intermittent sliding of the grill in the bottom of the door through which a stale heel of bread was pushed if he was lucky. It didn't feel as though he was often lucky. There wasn't always water, and when there was, it tasted like someone might have shat in it. He licked what he could from the dripping walls. The only other sound was a faint wet crackling that was usually followed by the sound of something being dragged along the floor. The boy quickly realised the wet crackling meant death.

Then, one day – if it was a day. He couldn't tell – he was woken by the clunk of a set of keys. Seconds later, the door to his cell was pushed open, and an oil lamp held high. Squinting in the sudden light, the boy wondered if it was his turn to be dragged along the floor. He wanted to tell the holder of the lamp that it must be a mistake – he wasn't dead yet.

But the guard didn't even look at him. Instead, he stepped aside and what looked to the boy to be some kind of large animal was shoved into the cell. The door slammed behind it, followed by the echo of keys being turned in the lock and gradually fading footsteps.

Fearfully, he peered at the bundle of rags motionless by the door, his heart thumping in time with the dripping water. At first, he thought the creature was dead, but eventually, it lifted its head and slowly got to its feet. The boy couldn't tell if it was a man or a beast. But the slowly shuffling footsteps told him the thing walked on two legs. A grunt and then the figure collapsed into the opposite corner. The boy pulled his legs up in an effort to make himself as small as possible and stared into the stygian darkness, straining his eyes in terror. But the figure didn't move and after what felt like hours, his head sank onto his knees as he drifted into a fitful doze, only to be woken by a snarl and a blast of fetid breath inches away from his face.

And that was when the boy truly began to believe he'd already gone to hell.

The boy endured the beatings by curling himself up into a ball and protecting his head with his arms. The only reason he survived was the simple fact that starvation will render even the biggest man weak. And it was a man. The boy discovered that when he woke to a warm stream of stinking urine hitting his face.

Unexpectedly, the brute did not steal every piece of bread shoved through the grill. Occasionally, he would toss a piece into the boy's corner. It was enough to keep his wasted body alive, though barely.

It was the unexpected arrival of another prisoner that saved his life.

From the moment the door opened, the boy knew things would be different. This time, in the lantern's light, he could clearly see it was a man. He was preceded by two guards dragging in a straw mattress. They didn't speak, but each held their free arm up against their nose and mouth to avoid breathing in the stench. They threw the mattress on the floor, up against the wall, before hurrying out.

Seconds later, the man was pushed, none too gently, into the room. The door clanged shut, and the key turned in the lock. But this time, before leaving, one of the guards hung the oil lamp just outside, allowing the weak light to shine through the small, barred window at the top of the door. It was the first time the boy had even noticed the opening was there.

The newcomer looked disdainfully around the dank room and held his arm over his nose, parroting the guards. Then he stepped carefully towards the mattress and sank down, his back against the wall. For the next few minutes, there was a taut silence. Then the creature, as the boy had begun to call him, pushed himself to his feet with a growl and staggered determinedly towards the man on the mattress, clearly intending to take the bed for himself.

'I would think very carefully before you make your next move.'

They were the first words the boy had heard in … truthfully; he did not know. He stared fearfully between his two cellmates as the creature stopped uncertainly.

'If I die at your hands, you will undoubtedly be praying for your own death – likely for days,' the man continued conversationally. 'But if you leave me be, I will keep you alive.' He turned his head towards the boy and added, 'Both of you.'

In the following weeks, the boy became stronger. The food, while not plentiful, came twice a day and even consisted of the dreamed of cheese. True to his word, the man shared his bounty between the three of them. The boy learned that the man's name was Pierre d'Ansouis. From his voice, it was clear he was not a *sans-culotte*. His clothes, though ragged, were well made, with fine cloth. He even had a coat - which he didn't share. Indeed, it seemed to the boy that the Monsieur complained about the cold even more than the stench.

The first time he heard the creature's voice was the first time he believed the brute to be truly human. That, and the grovelling towards d'Ansouis. It was almost impossible for the boy to believe this was the same creature who'd tormented him so. His name, or so he told the Monsieur, was Etienne Babin. He came from a village called Guisnes and was a cabinet maker by trade. He did not say why he had been thrown into prison, and the Monsieur didn't ask.

Neither man asked the boy anything at all.

Things continued in much the same vein for the next few months. For the first time the boy knew the difference between day and night and gradually his mind became clearer as he listened to the Monsieur speak – the man did love the sound of his own voice.

And then, one night, all hell broke loose.

## July 1808

The Albatross rocked gently at anchor, hidden by enormous cliffs on three sides. They'd arrived at dawn and expected to remain in hiding until their passenger arrived.

Captain Roan Carew was not good at waiting. He'd ordered the ship cleaned from forward to aft and now the brasses gleamed, and the deck had been freshly holystoned. Not that his sailors were any happier. Scrubbing the decks with the great slabs of gritty rock made for backbreaking labour. Only the promise of extra grog and a share of the prize money kept the complaining to a minimum.

Sighing, Roan stood on the quarterdeck and stared up at the French cliffs, so like their counterparts on the coast of Cornwall. From this angle, the narrow path they would bring the freed prisoner down was almost invisible. He didn't envy those who had to make the precarious descent in complete darkness, and he suspected that more than one man would lose his life this night. He only hoped that Pierre d'Ansouis wasn't one of them. There would be no coin for a body.

∼

The boy was woken by the shouting and then the sound of a gunshot. Terrified, he shrank against the wall. His eyes automatically flew towards the Monsieur who was climbing to his feet in apparent unconcern. He peered through the small window, then turned towards Babin. 'Come. Make sure you stay behind me.' His voice was low, but the boy didn't miss the suppressed excitement.

Without hesitation, Babin clambered to his feet and hurried to stand behind d'Ansouis. He asked no questions, his faith in the Monsieur complete. The boy watched wide-eyed from his corner.

Minutes later, there was a small *woomph* and the shouting became louder. Petrified, the boy climbed to his feet and watched as faces suddenly appeared at the small window. The sound of the key turning in the lock, then the door, was pushed open. 'Follow me, my lord.' The voice was urgent, and its owner turned away without waiting to see if d'Ansouis obeyed. The boy watched as the Monsieur immediately stepped out into the passageway, Babin at his heels. He glanced back into the cell, then, leaving the door wide open, disappeared from view.

The boy remained where he was for a few more terrified seconds until panic galvanised him and he sprinted after the disappearing lights.

# Seven

Panting in sheer dread at the thought of being left behind, the boy finally managed to catch up with the small group. He kept his distance, making sure to be just close enough to follow their lead, but far enough away to remain unnoticed. The boy feared that if he got left behind, he'd be lost forever. Doomed to wander the dark passageways until he starved.

After what seemed like hours, they finally broke free of the dark stone. Even though it was dark, the boy's eyes ran like he'd stared too long at the sun. He lost all sense of direction, simply following the group of men, sobbing under his breath with every step. It had been so long since he'd had any kind of exercise, and his body was weak and dehydrated. His bare feet hurt so badly, he felt like howling. Despite that, he laboured on. Only pausing when the group finally stepped off the edge of a cliff.

Fighting the urge to scream, the boy stepped to the verge and looked down. In the moon's light, he could just make out a path snaking down the steep face. The group of men were rapidly being swallowed up into the night. Swallowing, he stepped onto the narrow trail, slipping and sliding his way towards the bobbing lanterns.

He'd almost reached the point of not caring whether he lived or died. Indeed, he even thought briefly of throwing himself off the cliff and getting it over with. But when he heard the unmistakable sound of a body falling, accompanied by a shrill scream of terror, which ended in a horrible, dull thud, he pressed his back against the rock and moaned, fighting the urge to simply sit down.

He could still hear the voices in front of him, but they were getting fainter. If he remained still any longer, they would leave without him. Where exactly they were leaving to, the boy did not know and cared less. Anywhere that wasn't here. After wiping his arm across the line of snot running from his nose, he pressed his hand against the warm rock and began to slip and slide his way down the footpath. After another ten minutes or so, he caught sight of a faint light down in the water. Carefully peering over the edge, he screwed his eyes almost shut in an effort to see where the illumination was coming from. After a few seconds, his heart slammed against his ribs as he realised it was coming from a ship anchored in the deep water of the enclosed bay.

Weeping openly now, the boy recklessly skidded down the steep path, and finally reached a small, previously invisible jetty at the foot of the cliff, just as the Monsieur and Babin were climbing into a small skiff. The four men who'd conducted the rescue stood to one side. Evidently, they would not be accompanying them.

For a few seconds, the boy stood mute, until desperation loosened his tongue. 'Monsieur,' he croaked, using his voice for the first time in so long. One of the rescuers growled and stepped forward, clearly intending to throw the intruder into the water.

'Leave him be.' D'Ansouis' voice was harsh, and louder than the boy had ever heard it. Seconds later, an arm snaked out, the hand unceremoniously yanking him from the solid jetty into the pitching boat. The boy fell down into the hull and promptly curled up into a small ball, squeezing his eyes tightly shut. Seconds later, he felt the boat move.

Roan watched the skiff push off from the jetty. He was aware that one man had fallen to his death on the way down, but guessed the survivors would simply divide the poor sod's share of the coin between them.

He turned his attention to the rigging, slating against the mast. The wind was getting up, and it was imperative they cleared the bay as soon as possible to avoid being dashed against its rocky sides. Without waiting for the small boat to reach them, Roan began shouting orders. They needed to be away as soon as their *guest* was aboard.

Nearly ten minutes later, the foresails had been hoisted and the ship slowly began to turn. Roan was vaguely aware of the skiff being brought aboard, but all his attention was on the Albatross as she laboriously made her way out of the narrow gap between the bluffs at the mouth of the cove.

As they cleared the headland, Roan was able to relax slightly, gradually becoming aware of a commotion on the upper deck. Frowning, he gave his First Lieutenant charge and made his way towards the newcomers.

Newcomers, plural? As far as he was aware, it should simply have been one additional passenger. As he approached, Roan counted three. One, who despite his shabby appearance was clearly the Comte; a great, hulking brute who looked as though he might well be the nobleman's bodyguard; and lastly, a miserable, almost skeletal boy who he estimated had yet to reach ten summers, sobbing like the world had come to an end.

'What is the meaning of this?' Roan snapped, his patience nearing its end. 'Who are these?' He pointed at the brute and the child.

'They shared my cell,' d'Ansouis replied coolly. 'What would you have had me do – leave them? You know as well as I do, they would have been tortured until they'd begged to be allowed to die.'

Roan gritted his teeth. Everything the nobleman said was true. He looked over at the snivelling boy. 'Where are you from?' he asked in passable French. The lad stared at him in abject terror.

'I am certain he has no one,' the Comte intervened. 'Perhaps your charity might extend to a cabin boy?' He gave a shrug before adding, 'It's either that I think, or perhaps you would be better to throw him overboard now.'

'How is it you will not take him?' Roan barked, unaccountably riled at d'Ansouis's blithe comments.

'I have nothing,' the Comte answered, spreading his hands to better illustrate their emptiness. 'I go to plead my case with your countrymen simply to avoid ending up on the streets.'

Roan resisted the temptation to give a derogatory snort. The French Count would not end up in the gutter if the money that had been paid for his rescue was anything to go by.

'And your bodyguard?' the Captain asked, leaving the problem of the boy for a moment.

'He will stay with me.' D'Ansouis's voice brooked no argument. The boy he could throw overboard. Evidently, the hulking brute might yet prove useful.

Roan looked over at the shivering lad, and his heart contracted with a sudden pity. He turned to his second lieutenant. 'Give the boy some fresh clothes and a meal.' Watching the officer lay his hand on the skinny runt's shoulder, Roan had a sudden premonition that the foundling wasn't going anywhere any time soon.

'What's your name, boy?' he called as the lad was led away. The boy stopped and turned, scrubbing at his wet eyes with a dirty sleeve. He stared for a second, before twisting out of the second Lieutenant's grip and facing Roan. Then he bit his lip and lifted his right hand, fingers touching the side of his head. 'Tristan Bernart at your service, Sir.'

∼

Nicholas was not looking forward to the day. Indeed, his head currently felt as though it had been stuffed with wool. It wasn't often that circumstances kept him awake for most of the night, but the situation he'd found himself in was almost laughable. Almost.

He, Malcolm, Roan and Jamie had sat late into the night discussing how best to deal with the looming debacle. At length, after nearly depleting a bottle of brandy, the four men had concluded that there was no time to alter the plan and the unfortunate presence of two warring politicians on opposite sides of the proposed Reform bill would simply have to be managed. As would Dougal Galbraith.

The important thing was to get Tristan Bernart accepted into the underground faction, calling themselves the *Revisionists*. Ironically, the little-known group were advocates of reform, just as the current Prime Minister, Lord Grey. However, their methods to achieve it did not appear to include peaceful debate.

The radical group had been brought to the Duke's attention a year earlier, shortly after his return from Jennifer and Brandon's wedding.

On reaching Blackmore, he'd found a letter from his brother-in-law, Roan Carew, waiting for him. The missive had said very little, apart from the fact that he was looking forward to coming to Blackmore for their planned hunting and fishing weekend and expressing the hope that Jamie would be able to make it too.

Since no such invitation had been issued, either to Roan or Jamie, Nicholas swiftly surmised that the ex-sea captain had something important he wished to divulge in person and wanted Jamie to hear it too.

Ten days later, the three men spent two days *fishing* on the banks of Blackmore's large lake.

What Roan had to say was disquieting, to say the least.

Some years earlier, whilst he was still captain of the Albatross, Roan was ordered to anchor in secret in a little-known bay a few miles from Mont St. Michel. They'd been tasked to pick up a French nobleman by the name of Comte Pierre d'Ansouis.

The Comte had spent the last three years incarcerated in Napoleon's notorious *Bastille of the Seas* until freed by closet royalists.

Roan had been given no further information about the nobleman, aside from the fact that he apparently had influential English friends.

The whole rescue had gone almost according to plan, but instead of one escaped prisoner, there had been three. Roan had initially been inclined to toss the two interlopers overboard except that one of them was a mere boy. The other was a large hulk of a man who appeared to have set himself up as the Comte's man servant. D'Ansouis informed him they'd been housed in the same cell.

Five days later, the Albatross docked in Plymouth, and the Comte was whisked away. His unlikely *manservant* went too. The boy, however, had nowhere to go, and Roan resigned himself to the sudden unexpected acquisition of a cabin boy. The lad claimed to be ten years old and said his name was Tristan Bernart.

Despite Roan's reluctance to assume responsibility for the boy, the lad proved himself to be both bright and hardworking, and as Roan began to think about resigning his commission and settling down, he sent Tristan away to school, sensing the lad would be just as much an asset on dry land.

Indeed, over the following two decades, the former cabin boy proved himself beyond even Roan's expectations, and by the time Tristan was nearing thirty, the two had become partners in several extremely successful business ventures.

It was in the pursuit of one such venture that Tristan Bernart finally saw Pierre d'Ansouis again.

Or rather, the man who claimed to be Pierre d'Ansouis. Despite the intervening years, Tristan had no trouble recognising the man strolling down Regent Street in the company of two laughing young ladies, as Etienne Babin.

Reluctant to simply walk away from such an intriguing mystery, Tristan decided to look into the possible whereabouts of the genuine Pierre d'Ansouis. Based on his memories of Babin, he had no problem imagining the nobleman's demise by the former prisoner's hand, but despite extensive enquiries, he could find absolutely nothing. It was as if Babin had never existed.

Certain now that the real Comte d'Ansouis was pushing up daisies in some remote location, Tristan turned his attention to why Babin would risk the noose to take over the identity of a dispossessed French émigré. After extensive enquiries, the only thing he managed to unearth was a snippet of conversation overheard by a former disgruntled maid – and it had cost him a pretty penny.

Apparently, late one evening, she'd heard the Comte mention the word *Revisionists* to an unknown visitor. It meant nothing to Tristan, but nevertheless, he finally decided to take his findings to Roan.

The former sea captain had been involved in enough havey cavey business since leaving the Royal Navy to recognise there was something more amiss than a mistaken identity and promptly contacted the Duke of Blackmore.

While Nicholas had never heard the name mentioned before, Jamie had come across it on two earlier occasions. As far as the magistrate could ascertain, the *Revisionists* were a group of reformists with a particular grudge against those who were resisting change.

The three men agreed they should endeavour to find out as much as possible about the little-known group over the next few months in the hope of unearthing something tangible. Consequently, Jamie, in his official role, tasked the Bow Street Runners with observing any known crusaders of reform. Though much depleted since the advent of the new police force, the Runners nonetheless unearthed a rumour that these *Revisionists* thought to bypass the current arguments about reform raging between the Commons and the Lords by taking matters into their own hands.

But despite extensive investigation, the Runners could find no confirmed members of the supposedly radical group and no evidence at all of a connection between them and the bogus French Count.

There was, however, a palpable air of anxiety pervading the streets of London. A sense that something was coming. While the arguments for and against reform waged in the Houses of Commons and Lords, Nicholas, Jamie, Roan and Tristan began to believe something terrible was being planned.

It was time to take matters into their own hands.

# Eight

Nicholas elected to have breakfast in his study, and concerned about the pallor of his face as he left the bedchamber, Grace decided to join him. While she knew his pastiness was in part brandy induced, she was also well aware that the stress of their current predicament was taking its toll.

Because of the early hour, the hall was blessedly silent as Grace made her way down the stairs, and she was able to request a light repast be sent to his grace's study without meeting any of their guests. As she slipped into her husband's private sanctum, she breathed a sigh of relief. Experience told her that had she bumped into any of the family other than Jamie or Roan, she would not have escaped so easily.

Nicholas greeted her with a weary smile from behind his desk. 'Have you spoken with Roan or Jamie yet this morning?' she asked him lightly. The Duke shook his head and gave a pained smile.

'If their heads are anything like mine, they might yet have their heads in a bucket.'

'Mutton heads, all of you,' his wife muttered. 'I assume Malcolm too will be feeling a little worse for wear.'

'The man has a stomach of iron,' Nicholas growled. 'I doubt he's feeling the least bit shabby. I'm expecting his disgustingly cheerful face to show itself imminently.'

'Well, hopefully, not before breakfast,' Grace responded, seating herself in one of the two chairs fronting the large fireplace. In truth, she was trying not to laugh.

'I'm not sure I could eat anything.' Nicholas pulled a face as he climbed to his feet and went over to join her.

'I asked Mrs Higgins to put together a cleansing tincture,' his wife answered, not without sympathy. Then she gave a small, wicked grin and added, 'I didn't think you'd want me to ask Agnes.'

Nicholas shuddered and sat down in the chair opposite. 'Clearly something else has happened to drive the four of you so deeply into your cups,' she guessed. 'Are you going to tell me?'

Before the Duke could answer, there was a knock at the door. Moments later, a maid came in with a large tray, which she set between them.

'Thank you, Mary. Could you inform Mrs Tenner that if anyone asks our whereabouts, we will see them at lunch.' The small maid kept her head down and bobbed a curtsy before backing hurriedly out of the room.

'After all these years, I still find that so difficult,' Grace sighed, leaning forward to uncover a plate of freshly baked scones. 'All the bowing and scraping. It still feels wrong. I daresay I'll always be a vicar's daughter at heart.'

Nicholas took the plate she held out, his appetite coming back at the sight of the hot buttered scone, still fresh from the oven. 'Do not style yourself so, love,' he grinned. 'You're certainly not just any vicar's daughter. Your father's reputation has travelled the length and breadth of Great Britain.'

'And that's a good thing?' Grace questioned tartly. 'Here, drink this before you begin eating.' She held out a large glass of what looked disturbingly like something he'd removed from a pond as a boy.

Nicholas raised his eyebrows. 'You want me to drink that?'

'Unless you'd prefer me to tell Mrs Tenner you refused.'

The high and mighty duke grimaced and obediently held out his hand.

'So, what's happened to put you all so deep in your cups?' Grace quizzed him again as she handed him the glass.

Scowling, Nicholas swallowed the housekeeper's concoction in two gulps. When he'd recovered from the bitter taste, he told her of Wellington and Grey's unexpected visits.

'Why the devil did you invite them both?' Grace stared at him, appalled.

'I had no choice,' he responded, picking up his scone. 'To leave either off the guest list would have been seen as a slight and almost certainly misconstrued, given the current climate. I had no idea they would *both* be thick skinned or bloody minded enough to attend. Clearly, a catastrophic error on my part.'

'I think we are looking at two men possessing both traits in full,' Grace retorted. 'And with Dougal Galbraith here at the same time...' She trailed off and climbed to her feet. Adding, 'I need a sherry,' to Nicholas's enquiring look.

'It's my hope that your father will take Galbraith off our hands. I sent him a missive yesterday evening.' Far from reassuring her as he'd believed, his statement elicited a small moan, and she quickly poured and swallowed her sherry.

'Once the two arrive, it will fall on me to keep the peace, so at that point I will have to leave the Comte to Jamie, Roan, Malcolm and Tristan,' Nicholas continued as she resumed her seat. 'D'Ansouis will be arriving tomorrow, so we have two days to bring Tristan to his attention without the distraction of our two warring politicians.'

'That's providing he's not actually here for the two politicians,' Grace retorted, voicing her husband's unspoken fear.

He opened his mouth to respond, but was interrupted by a knock on the door. As predicted, Malcolm walked in full of the joys of spring.

'By the look on yer face, lass, Nick's told you the dire news,' the valet commented mildly, leaning down to pinch a scone.

Nicholas raised his eyebrows. 'Doesn't Felicity feed you?'

'Aye, but why waste our provisions when I can just as easily eat yours.'

Grace grinned up at him, then climbed to her feet and kissed his grizzled cheek. 'Will Felicity be joining us over the weekend?'

Malcolm gave a short laugh. 'Not if she can avoid it without seeming ill-mannered.'

'Tell her I will be entirely put out if she does not show her face,' Grace retorted, only half joking.

'Aye, she kens lass.' Malcolm chuckled and patted the Duchess's shoulder as he would a slightly troublesome child. 'I'm sure she can be persuaded tae be there at yer shoulder like always.' He turned to the Duke. 'What time are we expecting Tristan for his set down?'

'I told him eleven,' Nicholas replied. 'Jamie too, if he's managed to get his head off the pillow.'

'Unlicked cubs, the both o' ye,' Malcolm grinned. 'We still have five minutes then. I'll have another scone.'

Just seconds later, there came the expected knock at the door. Before Malcolm had the chance to open it, Jamie's wan face appeared. 'Mother o' God, ye look like ye've been dug up.' Malcolm gave another chuckle, as the door was pushed fully open, and Jamie was followed into the room by his wife.

'The chucklehead confessed all while in his cups,' Prudence declared waspishly, shutting the door behind her. 'In the future, your grace, you would do well to ensure your co-conspirators keep a clear head while plotting nefarious schemes without sharing said schemes with their wives.' She looked pointedly at her sister. 'Though clearly not all wives have been kept in the dark.'

Grace looked at Prudence in exasperation. 'It would have been a little difficult to hide, since the nefarious scheme in question is taking place in my house.'

'I know that,' Prudence relented with a grin. 'Are there any scones left?'

'I'm beginning to think we might as well have the whole family in on the damn thing,' Nicholas grated. 'I...' He paused whatever he was going to say as a knock sounded on the door.

Seconds later Roan pushed it open and walked in, looking none the worse for his overindulgence.

'How is it you're not looking like a seven-day-old corpse?' Jamie managed indignantly.

Roan grinned at him. 'After years of drinking grog, one has a tendency to develop a stomach of leather.'

Another knock. 'Hopefully that will be Tristan,' Nicholas muttered. Pushing himself up out of the chair, he took a more formal position behind his desk and barked, 'Come!'

The door opened, and, as he'd hoped, Tristan Bernart stood on the threshold. Stepping forward, the footman gave a deep bow. 'Shut the door,' Nicholas ordered, his voice both loud and sharp in case someone should be listening. Once the room was secure, Tristan raised his eyebrows at the number of people in the room.

'Don't ask,' Nicholas stated in a low tone, just as another knock sounded. Swearing in vexation, the Duke got back to his feet and ordered all but Tristan to stay out of sight. 'Whoever it is, I'll get rid of them,' he announced, walking round the desk towards the door.

The knock came again, more urgently this time, but as he raised his hand to lift the latch, it was flung open to reveal his father-in-law. The two men regarded each other in surprise for a moment, then the Reverend, threw his hands in the air, and declared loudly, 'I might well have the Almighty on my side, but even He knows that keeping Dougal Galbraith out of mischief for four whole days is going to take a bit more than divine intervention.'

The Duke stared at him in silence for a second before uttering, 'Augustus,' through gritted teeth and stepping aside. Bristling with righteous indignation, the Reverend marched into the study, only to stop and frown at the unexpected addition of six people. 'You having a deuced rout?' he demanded, the unvoiced, *without me*, left hanging in the air.

Briefly closing his eyes in a *Lord give me strength* gesture, Nicholas swiftly closed the door, and strode back to his desk. Once behind it, he looked round at his co-conspirators and grated, 'And then there were eight.' Silence reigned for the briefest of seconds, before he added a clipped, 'Malcolm, a brandy if you please,' just as another knock sounded on the door.

This time, his expletive was a little more colourful. With a wince, Grace hurriedly climbed to her feet. 'Let me,' she declared as the knock came again. Seconds later, she pulled open the door to reveal the very last person she expected to see on the other side.

Dipping a quick curtsy, Roseanna mumbled, 'Good morning, Aunt Grace,' before stepping into the room and blurting, 'Uncle Nicholas, forgive me for interrupting, but I think someone is planning to murder you.'

If Roseanna hadn't been so anxious, she might have found the look of disbelief on the Duke's face quite humorous, and even she knew that his grace rarely found himself lost for words.

As the silence lengthened, Roseanna abruptly realised that her uncle was not alone in the room with Tristan as she'd believed. Avoiding the footman's gaze, she looked around, realising there were actually another six people in the room. From the conversation she'd overheard in the kitchen garden, she could understand the presence of Uncle Jamie and Malcolm – even Aunt Grace. But she certainly hadn't been expecting her Aunt Prudence, or, worse still, her grandfather, who was currently regarding her with a narrow-eyed, thoughtful expression.

'I...I'm sorry, your grace,' she faltered. 'I didn't mean to interrupt anything. Err...would you prefer me to come back later?'

'I dinnae think the tale ye have tae tell will wait, lass,' Malcolm responded firmly. 'I ken the Duke will consider an attempted murder to his person of the utmost importance.'

Nicholas leaned back against his chair and schooled his face into something a little more reassuring. 'Why don't you go back to the beginning Rosie,' he suggested. 'Tell me everything that's happened.'

Unexpectedly, she felt herself relax slightly at his use of her nickname. Hesitantly, keeping her eyes on her uncle, she recounted what she'd heard. Naturally, she didn't tell the Duke that she'd been exploring the library with a view to eavesdropping on his conversation – just said that she had awakened early and thought to look for a book to read.

'And you didn't see these two persons?' Nicholas quizzed her when she finished speaking.

Roseanna shook her head. 'I did think to go out into the corridor, but in truth, they had me a little scared.'

'And well ye didn't lass. Can you remember, word for word, what they actually said about their intentions?'

'They were clearly looking for something,' Roseanna reiterated. She creased her brow and thought for a moment. 'They actually said, *It has to be here somewhere*. Then a few minutes later I heard, *We daren't stay any longer, the maid will be coming in. At the end of the day...*' she paused and reddened before finishing, '*as long as the bastard's dead.*'

'So, they didn't actually use his grace's name?' Malcolm pressed. Roseanna started to shake her head, then paused. 'They used the name Sinclair, as in *Sinclair wouldn't have put it anywhere else*, when they discussed what they were looking for.'

Jamie swore softly and climbed to his feet. 'Do you think d'Ansouis is planning something?' he grated. 'Surely he wouldn't risk committing murder while he's staying in the same deuced house.' He turned to Roseanna. 'Did they give any indication of time, Rosie?'

Roseanna shook her head. 'Whatever it was they were looking for, they expected it to be under lock and key. In truth, I don't think they held out much hope of finding it. They seemed more worried about leaving any trace of their snooping...' she hesitated, staring down at her slippers, then seconds later, looked up, her face brightened as she remembered something else. 'They said they'd be able to tell *his nibs* they tried.'

# Nine

'Do you have any new servants?' Prudence asked.

Nicholas instinctively looked towards his wife. 'Several,' Grace supplied. 'Though most of them will be here only for the duration of the garden party.'

'Do we risk questioning them?' Jamie quizzed. 'If any are connected to d'Ansouis, there's a strong possibility he might guess we're on to him.'

Nicholas shook his head wearily. 'I can't even begin to imagine what the rogues were looking for. In truth, I'm not sure there's anything in my study that might be of particular value to a would-be traitor. But while we don't want to alert the Comte, we'll have to keep a sharp eye on all the staff who've been at Blackmore for less than six months.'

'I think a year,' Jamie ground out. 'These bastards play a long game.'

Nicholas nodded, then swore softly. 'I really didn't want this to become a damn circus,' he grimaced, 'but we don't have eyes in the back of our heads, and after what Rosie has just told us, it's clear we have much more to worry about than trying to slip one of our own into an underground radical group.

'If these two thieves are in the pay of the Comte, he could well be considering something untoward. And though we haven't yet voiced it, we cannot discount the possibility that it is not my person he wishes to harm, but someone else attending the house party.' He grimaced and ran his fingers through his hair in frustration. 'And now, with the unexpected attendance of two politicians on opposite sides of the reform bill...' He paused and closed his eyes briefly. 'We cannot assume that the Comte - or anyone else, for that matter, is unaware that Wellington and Grey will be here. Both the blockheads' decision to attend might have been at the eleventh hour, but if the conspirators have eyes and ears in their respective households...' He trailed off and shrugged.

'The *Revisionists* might consider it too good an opportunity to miss,' Jamie finished.

Nicholas nodded into the subsequent silence, before adding, 'I think we have no alternative but to seek the aid of those we know we can trust.'

'Ye'll involve the whole family, laddie?' Malcolm's voice was incredulous.

'Just my brothers-in-law,' the Duke clarified.

Grace, Prudence, and Roseanna made identical sounds of protest, only to subside when Nicholas uttered the word, 'Patience.' And he wasn't talking about the emotion.

He turned his attention to the Reverend. 'Augustus, I will leave Galbraith in your hands. I know that you feel in need of some assistance, and I'm certain we can avail upon various members of the family to help you ensure he stays out of mischief – specifically out of Wellington and Grey's path...'

'That's all very well, if you're simply asking me to keep him well away from the deuced politicians, but if you're looking to keep him away from the party and everyone attending it, including would-be assassins...' He trailed off before giving a small cough and looking sideways towards his granddaughter. 'The thing is,' he added. 'I can't be running around trying to find people to give me a hand when they have a spare few minutes. What I need is a person or persons specifically chosen to help me keep an eye on Dougal while the old addlepate's under your roof. Someone who doesn't have much of an interest in fripperies. It's no good assigning me someone too ripe and ready.'

The Duke raised his eyebrows. 'I'm surprised you haven't already enlisted Percy's aid,' he commented drily. 'He's been by your side throughout all your other high jinks.'

Augustus Shackleford bristled and drew himself up. 'My so-called *high jinks*, your grace, have, I believe, put a rub in the way of more than one blackguard's plans. And since it appears that we may have several such characters here in Blackmore, you might find yourself glad of my assistance.'

In truth, Nicholas couldn't argue with the Reverend's words – however unconventional the clergyman's methods might have been over the years. 'You're right, of course, Augustus,' he conceded, bending his head. 'Please accept my apologies. I meant no offence. However, I cannot imagine Percy refusing to assist you on this occasion.'

Reverend Shackleford hmphed and gave a small cough. 'The fact of the matter is,' he began uncomfortably, on this particular occasion, 'I would prefer to enlist the aid of someone other than my curate.'

'Have you had a falling out, Father?' Grace interrupted, her voice radiating concern.

'Not at all,' the Reverend retorted hastily. He paused and fidgeted with his cassock. 'It's just that...' Oh, devil take it – how was he to explain without casting aspersions on the old Scot's moral character?

Fortunately, Malcolm, being the only other person in the room who'd witnessed Dougal Galbraith in action, came to the rescue. 'I'm assuming ye wish to minimise any bad influence on young Finn,' the valet stated bluntly.

The Reverend nodded in relief. 'Exactly,' he declared. 'I think the less time those two get to spend together, the better things will be for both the lad and Percy. And if we do indeed have a conspiracy taking place under our very noses, I think the lad will be best kept well away.'

'Goodness, Papa, is your conscience finally coming to the fore now you're getting closer to meeting your maker?' Prudence gave a mischievous wink, ignoring her father's scowl as she tried to lighten the sombre mood. 'I don't think you have anything to worry about,' she continued. 'I doubt the Almighty's even remotely ready for you yet.'

'So, what do you suggest, Augustus?' Jamie asked before his wife dug herself into an even deeper hole. Not that Prudence had ever had a problem with putting her foot in it. She was only slightly better than her sister Patience in that regard.

Augustus Shackleford glared at his daughter, who grinned unrepentantly, before giving an indignant sniff and deliberately addressing his next words to the Duke. 'Might I suggest, your grace, that since Roseanna and I are both now unfortunately involved in this deuced business, she is the perfect candidate to act as my second-in-command in the ongoing battle to keep Dougal Galbraith firmly on the path of righteousness – at least while he's here in Blackmore.'

Roseanna stared at her grandfather in horrified silence. While she had no problem with eschewing *fripperies,* as the Reverend had called the proposed routs and games, this was not the alternative she had in mind. It would involve spending almost the entire time with her grandparent. Up to now, the number of hours she'd spent alone in his company since the day she was born amounted to less than a handful. Indeed, she couldn't remember the last time they'd held a conversation – if ever.

For some reason, her eyes flew to Tristan Bernart. The footman had been conspicuously silent since her arrival, and his expression was now carefully impassive. She felt a sudden flare of irritation at his unreadable countenance before remembering that he could not possibly have an opinion on her relationship with her grandfather, since he didn't know anything about her at all. How strange it was that she felt as though she'd known him forever. Perhaps it was the altercations that had characterised their two meetings – not unlike the bickering she was accustomed to with members of her family.

She became aware that her Aunt Grace was speaking. Flushing, Roseanna hurriedly abandoned her musing and looked over at her aunt.

'Perhaps you can tell us your thoughts on your grandfather's proposal.' The Duchess's words were concerned, and Roseanna realised that her feelings must have been obvious from her expression.

The young woman looked around the study, noting varying degrees of sympathy. Clearly, everyone in the room, with the exception of Tristan, had had a lot more dealings with the Reverend than she had. Her eyes finally settled on her grandfather, who was nodding at her enthusiastically.

It was true, she'd had very little to do with the Reverend throughout her childhood, but she'd grown up with the tales of his escapades. This was an opportunity for her to finally get to know the man behind the myth, and mayhap, while she was about it, she'd be able to assist in their other, much bigger problem since there was every possibility that she might have occasion to hear and recognise the voices of the two men in the Duke's study.

Much better than playing croquet and talking to strangers.

Roseanna did not talk much during luncheon, but since that was the usual state of affairs, nobody remarked on it. Afterwards, she turned down a game of croquet with her cousins on the pretext of taking Trixie for a walk. She told herself that her excuse wasn't really a complete plumper since she and her grandfather had agreed to meet up in Blackmore's orchard and Rosie intended to take the little dog with her. Once there, they would endeavour to plan their strategy.

As she made her way through the kitchen garden, Roseanna felt a little sick. Nothing like this had ever happened to her before. Indeed, she was only now realising just how sheltered her life had been. While her grandfather's reputation was almost legendary, his exploits had always simply been stories she'd listened to, wide eyed.

That said, she had been on the periphery of some excitement not two months earlier when a dreadful man from the Americas had tried to kidnap her step cousin, Mercedes. Her grandfather had been in the thick of that havey cavey business as well. Truly, she was beginning to think the Reverend attracted trouble like bees to nectar. She determinedly swallowed her apprehension. At least the next few days were unlikely to be dull.

The weather was hotter than the day before, and Roseanna was glad to finally reach the welcoming coolness of the orchard. She was a little early and after finding herself a shady place to sit; she decided to take a chance and let Trixie off her lead. At first, she watched apprehensively as the little dog dashed from tree to tree. If the little madam decided to take off, there would be no way to catch her. However, Rosie soon realised there was no need to worry. Clearly, Trixie knew exactly which side of her bread was buttered and, after a mad few minutes, flopped happily down next to her new mistress.

'Be she yer dog, missus?' The disembodied voice startled her. Jumping to her feet, she looked around wildly.

'What be her name?' This time she realised the voice was coming from directly above her. Looking up, she spied a pair of feet dangling from a branch. 'What on earth are you doing?' Rosie gasped. 'Whoever you are, you must come down at once before you break your neck.'

'Ah dinnae think so, milady,' the voice scoffed. 'Ah've climbed tae the very top wi nae problem.' A face appeared through the leaves, clearly belonging to a young boy. He leaned forward, one hand holding nonchalantly onto the gnarled limb above him. Roseanna gasped as his whole body almost slid off the branch he was sitting on. Next to her, Trixie danced about in excitement.

Recognising that the boy had obviously done this many times before, Rosie swallowed her fear as a sudden thought occurred to her. 'Are you Finn?' she asked.

He stared down at her for a second before answering. 'Aye. Who be ye, missus?'

'I'm Rosie,' she answered promptly. 'I'm staying at Blackmore for the weekend.'

'Be ye the Duke's guest? Be ye gaun tae the party?'

Roseanna nodded, her heart jumping back into her throat as the branch swayed alarmingly above her. 'Why don't you come down?' she suggested. 'It's very difficult to speak with you with my neck craned up so.' The boy thought for a second, then his head disappeared, followed by the hanging feet. The entire tree shivered, and moments later, a boy of about eight stepped out from behind the tree. His pockets were bulging with early apples, giving a clear indication of what he'd been up to. He immediately got down onto his knees to fuss over Trixie, who promptly rolled onto her back. 'What be her name?' he asked again.

'I call her Trixie,' Roseanna answered, smiling as she watched him gently stroke the dog's exposed belly. Clearly, he was familiar with dogs. 'Are you supposed to be here?' she went on when he finally looked up.

'Ah be a guid friend tae 'is grace,' the boy boasted importantly. 'Ah keep ma eyes on things, roond aboot lest he be robbed.'

'I can imagine there are many who would steal the Duke's apples,' Rosie replied, her voice carefully neutral, though she was trying hard not to laugh.

'Aye.' He nodded seriously, completely ignoring his bulging pockets. 'Ah be gaun tae the party,' he told her. 'Wi' ma Mam an' Da.' His face darkened before he added, 'Mam sez ah've tae hae a bath first.' He shook his head sorrowfully. Clearly, this was dire news.

'Tare an' hounds, Finn Noon. How many times have I told you not to help yourself to the Duke's apples?' The booming voice of the Reverend took them both by surprise. Seconds later, a ball of fur came charging across the clearing to throw herself into the boy's arms.

'Flossy!' Finn cried in delight, allowing himself to fall backwards as the little dog danced on his front. The two wrestled for a few seconds as Trixie watched in bemusement.

'Remove those apples from your pockets immediately, young man, or I'll be telling his grace and he'll put you in his dungeons with nothing but bread and water until you're too old to climb a deuced tree.'

Finn sat up and grinned unrepentantly. 'Guid day Revren,' he chirped. 'This is Rosie. She be gaun tae 'is grace's party an aw.' Climbing to his feet, he tipped the apples out of his pocket and onto the ground – all but one, which he bit into with relish. Then, with a brief bow, he took to his heels.

Roseanna glanced sideways at her grandfather to see his reaction. To her surprise, he was looking after the boy with exasperated affection. 'So, that was Finn,' she commented. 'I can understand why you might not wish to expose him to any undesirable influences.' Her voice was dry, and the Reverend regarded her thoughtfully.

'So, you've a sense of humour, girl,' he observed. 'That's all to the good. Believe me, you'll need it after spending four days with old Dougal Galbraith.'

Tristan sat with the canteen of silver cutlery in front of him. He'd been at it for over an hour, but so far, all he'd managed to clean was half a dozen fish knives. At this rate, he'd still be sitting here in the early hours. As he polished, he allowed his mind to go back over the meeting in the Duke's study. Lady Roseanna's unladylike eavesdropping had certainly put the cat amongst the pigeons. The entire business had been tricky enough without adding a conspiracy within a conspiracy to the mix. In truth, it sounded like some kind of Canterbury tale, but given that his own past read like some kind of gothic periodical, Tristan knew that fact could occasionally be stranger than fiction.

He knew that the last few members of the family were due to arrive later on that day. The Duke had expressed the hope that they would all arrive before dinner so that he could get his brothers-in-law alone without their wives. Clearly, his intention was to both enlighten them and request their help over the port. Tristan chuckled to himself as he thought back to Nicholas Sinclair's strict words to the Duchess that under no circumstances was she to share the whole smoky business with her sisters. Obviously, one of them was already involved, and Tristan had caught the look the two ladies exchanged before they left the room.

What he knew of the Duke of Blackmore's extended family had mainly come from gossip, especially less than complimentary descriptions of the Sisters' rebelliousness - not to mention their father who was the least reverend-like Reverend he'd ever met.

And it looked as though the next generation were also possessed of the same wilful traits. He thought back to the determined face of the Duchess's niece. Roseanna was a pretty name - though the Duke had called her Rosie. No doubt it was a family nickname. Somehow, the less formal version suited her.

As he plied his rag, Tristan tasted the sound of her name on his tongue, then abruptly brought himself up short. There would never be a time when he would get to call her that to her face. He might not be a footman in truth, but he *was* a bastard, and that was the only title he was ever likely to hold, no matter how far he'd come in the world.

# Ten

'I am so dreadfully sorry, Father. Dougal ambushed us when we were leaving, giving us no time to think up an excuse.'

'Ah'll dae everything in my power tae make sure the bampot behaves himself, yer grace,' her husband added. 'Ah'll be sure tae keep him entertained until the other guests hae gone.'

At that moment, Nicholas wouldn't have cared if they'd brought the devil himself with them. He was simply glad to see his only daughter. Stepping forward, he enfolded her in a tight hug. It had been too long.

Jennifer turned next to her mother, with both women weeping openly as they embraced. As Nicholas looked over at Brendon, he found himself suddenly fighting a sudden insane urge to laugh. The poor man looked as though he was about to end it all. He smiled ruefully at the young Scot. 'It's good to see you Brendon, and under normal circumstances, your father too. It is entirely my fault that we have two politicians here from opposite sides of the house, but if they think to use Blackmore as a cockfighting ring, they will find themselves on the way back to London – no matter how important they think they are.'

The four of them were in the small drawing room, grabbing an illicit moment together before the rest of the family realised Jenny and Brendon had arrived. Peter knew they were here, and after giving his sister a fierce hug, he'd bought them some time by whisking Dougal off on an impromptu tour of the house. Naturally, their presence would be noted soon enough.

'We want you both to enjoy your stay here, politics be damned,' Grace added as Jennifer seated herself between her parents, while Brendon took the chair opposite. 'And anyway, your grandfather has very kindly offered to look after Dougal whilst the house is full.'

Jennifer raised her eyebrows in alarm. 'Is that wise, Mama?'

'Well, I would be a little concerned,' her mother admitted, 'but your cousin Roseanna has offered to help him.'

Jennifer cast her mother a narrow-eyed look, and Grace felt her stomach roil. Her daughter was anything but stupid. 'Why on earth would Rosie do such a thing?'

'Oh darling, you know how she hates having to mix with crowds of strangers,' Grace answered carefully. 'So, she offered her services.' Both facts were perfectly true. 'What time do Tony and George expect to be here?' she added, hoping to change the subject.

'They were intending to leave as soon as Henry had had his lunch,' Jennifer answered, so I'd imagine another hour or so.' She grinned. 'He's a gorgeous little boy, but such a handful. I'm certain he's going to be another Grandpapa.'

'God help us,' Nicholas retorted fervently.

'Have Mercy and Nate arrived yet?' Jennifer asked in turn.

'Not half an hour ago,' the Duchess responded, inwardly sighing with relief that Jenny had let the matter of Roseanna drop.

Before Jennifer could say anything further, there was a loud knock on the door, accompanied by what sounded like stifled giggles. Nicholas sighed. Clearly, their brief sojourn was at an end. 'I think your accomplices might well be aware of your arrival,' he commented drily.

Jennifer gave a broad smile that tugged straight at his heart strings before throwing out her arms to encompass them both in a tight hug. 'It's so good to be home, she murmured, before jumping to her feet and holding out her hand to her husband. 'Are you game to meet the horde?' she quizzed him impishly.

He grinned up at her before climbing to his feet and taking her hand. 'Wi you, lass, ah'm game tae face anythin'.'

~

Percy Noon was troubled. He'd known Reverend Shackleford long enough to know when his superior was keeping things from him. The telltale fidgeting, and hmphs, not to mention the Reverend's habit of avoiding eye contact.

Simply put, despite his recklessness, Augustus Shackleford was really not very good at shamming it.

Naturally, the curate respected the Reverend's desire to keep his own counsel, but in truth, it did smart a little. Percy was accustomed to being fully involved in the clergyman's troubles, and while he'd oft told his wife Lizzy that being constantly dragged into affairs that were none of his business was wearying in the extreme, he was honest enough to recognise that without the added excitement the Reverend provided, life was actually rather humdrum.

'Not that humdrum is bad,' he hastened to reassure Lizzy, 'especially if we want to set a good example for Finn.'

'You think humdrum is good for Finn?' Lizzy had queried.

'Well, I...' Percy stuttered to a halt, frowning.

Lizzy suppressed a smile at her husband's expression. 'If the lad's life becomes too *humdrum*,' she went on, he'll just create his own entertainment. I never thought I'd say this, Percy, but Augustus Shackleford is good for the boy. Keeps the lad on his toes.'

Percy drank his tea in thoughtful silence. 'You know, now you come to mention it,' he commented at length, 'it's not only me Reverend Shackleford is avoiding. It's Finn too.' The curate put his half-finished dish of tea onto the table. 'And it all started when he told me Dougal Galbraith was coming.'

'Do you think he doesn't want you to meet him?' Lizzy asked. 'Why on earth would he wish to keep the two of you apart?'

Percy didn't answer immediately, thinking about the Reverend's discomfort when he suggested inviting Dougal Galbraith for dinner. 'I don't think it is me,' he said eventually. 'I think it's Finn.'

Lizzy frowned in confusion. 'Is he worried that seeing Dougal will make Finn homesick for Scotland?'

Percy shook his head. 'No, it's not that. If that was the case, he'd tell me.'

'Well, in fairness, it's not like Reverend Shackleford to keep things to himself unless he has good reason,' Lizzy said, just as the door opened to admit their adopted son.

'Did ye ken that the Revren and a lady are gaun tae be keeping Dougal Galbraith oot o' trouble,' the lad declared excitedly. 'An ah'm gaunae help 'em.'

Percy raised his eyebrows. 'He asked you to help him?'

'Nae,' Finn scoffed. 'Ah heard 'em. The Revren tellt the lady Dougal'll turn ma heid.' He gave a baffled shrug. 'Ah'm nae a wee one, and ah can turn ma own heid.'

Percy looked over at Lizzy in sudden comprehension. 'I think perhaps the Reverend thinks Dougal might be a bad influence,' he said carefully after a few seconds.

'Really?' Finn responded excitedly. 'That be better.'

By six p.m. that evening, the whole family had finally arrived, and the noise was such that one would be forgiven for thinking there were as many dogs as people. In addition to Trixie and Flossy, there was Brendon's Fergus, Anthony's Nelson and Nathaniel's Ruby. Since her grandfather had suggested he introduce her to Dougal Galbraith that evening, Roseanna decided to give Trixie the opportunity to get to know her doggie cousins before changing for dinner.

The Duke had decreed that once their other guests began arriving, the dogs would no longer be given the free run of the house, and watching the current pandemonium, Rosie could only agree with his decision.

The first guest arriving on the morrow would be the Comte d'Ansouis. Roseanna felt an anxious tremor at the thought that the man could be a traitor. Uncle Nicholas had made it very clear she was to stay well away from the Frenchman. She didn't think it would be especially difficult. By all accounts, he was even older than the Duke and hopefully unlikely to take any interest in a gaggle of young, immature women fresh from the schoolroom. She was, however, relieved that soon her father would be aware of the situation. She didn't know if the Duke would tell him about her eavesdropping – in truth; she hoped not. She wasn't especially proud of what she'd done, and as the day had worn on, she began to wonder if she'd made a mountain out of a molehill.

Having spent the last hour catching up with her aunts and cousins, she was now sitting on a bench, slightly apart, as was her wont. Smiling, she watched the dogs dash around the immaculate lawn, wincing as they cut across the flower beds. At this rate, Uncle Nicholas would need to replant them all. But then, neither he nor Aunt Grace had ever set much store on appearances except when forced.

'Would you care for some lemonade, my lady?' Without looking, Roseanna knew exactly who had spoken, and her heart slammed against her ribs. She glanced over at Tristan Bernart, looking almost impossibly handsome in his livery. His hair shone almost blue in the early evening sun, and as his eyes met hers, she felt again the disturbing sensation deep in her stomach.

'Yes, please,' she mumbled as he held out the tray. After taking a glass, she expected him to simply walk away, but instead, he laid the tray on the table and turned towards her.

Looking up at him, she felt her face begin to flame. Truly, she wasn't equipped to deal with handsome members of the opposite sex – gentlemen or otherwise.

'May I speak plainly, my lady?' he murmured.

Unexpectedly, her anxiety lessened as he spoke. He sounded…hesitant.

'You have always done so in our previous meetings, as I recall,' she heard herself saying. He did not immediately continue, and after a few seconds, she looked sideways at him. His eyes were no longer on her, but the fifteen or so other members of the family who were dotted around. 'Will you be taking your dog out for a walk after dinner?' he finally murmured, picking up his tray.

'I…I would expect so,' she answered cautiously.

'Would you meet me at the entrance to the herb garden?' His voice was urgent now, even as he continued to stare out over the lawn.

For a second, Rosie thought she'd misheard, but as he glanced down, his gaze curiously intent, she found herself nodding. 'What time?' she murmured, wondering if she'd gone mad.

'I believe dinner will be early again this evening,' he answered, giving her a short bow. 'Shall we say ten thirty?' He waited only until she gave a brief nod, then strode towards her cousins. Flustered, she watched him stop to speak to Mercy, Tory and Jennifer, who'd been as thick as thieves since their arrival. Seconds later, Trixie came running up, only to flop down, panting. Bending down to fuss the exhausted dog, Rosie found it difficult to breathe. Her heart was galloping, and she felt curiously light-headed. What the devil was she doing agreeing to meet a man she barely knew alone in the dark? Was she truly addled?

Then she took herself to task. Whatever it was that Tristan wished to say, it was undoubtedly to do with the discussion in the study. There was nothing about his mannerisms that spoke of romantic intention.

Likely, he had something he felt she should be aware of. He could even be passing on a message from the Duke. She took a sip of her lemonade. She didn't really believe that. If her Uncle Nicholas wished to tell her something, he would speak to her himself.

But whatever it was, the footman had deemed it important enough to ask her to risk her reputation. She suppressed a sudden urge to laugh. If someone had told her a week ago that she would be agreeing to a clandestine meeting with a handsome fictitious footman, she'd have thought them addled.

Frankly, so much had happened, she hardly recognised herself.

'Rosie, are you coming to get ready for dinner?' She spied Francesca coming towards her. Nodding with a smile, Rosanna bent down to put Trixie back on her lead and stood up to wait for her sister.

'Are you well, dearest?' Frankie was looking at her with concern. Though she knew better than to try to cajole Rosie into joining their games, it didn't stop her from worrying about her twin sitting alone.

'I'm fine.' Rosie pushed away her misgivings and smiled brightly at her twin, linking their arms. 'What are you thinking to wear this evening? Your blue dress or mayhap the orange?'

# Eleven

'May I present Dougal Galbraith. Dougal, this is my granddaughter, Roseanna.'

Roseanna looked at the scrawny man in front of her in slight alarm. Truly, he looked as though a puff of wind would blow him over. 'Good evening, Mr Galbraith. It's a pleasure to make your acquaintance. Please, call me Rosie.' She dipped into a brief curtsy and smiled politely.

He looked her up and down for a second before turning to her grandfather. 'Has this lass been gaen the job o' keepin' me oot o' mischief, along wi' ye, then Augustus?'

The Reverend gave a light laugh which ended in a cough. 'Come now, Dougal. It's not like that at all. The Duke simply thought you would enjoy seeing a little of Devonshire rather than merely standing around making polite conversation with strangers.'

'Aye, well, he has the right o' it. Boring bloody sassenachs the lot o' 'em.'

'Why did you come, Sir?' Roseanna asked curiously.

Leaning forward, the Scot gave her a toothless grin. 'Look o'er there at ma boy. He be the one who looks like he be suckin' on a lemon.' Rosie looked over at Jennifer's husband, Brendon. He was staring over at them anxiously. She turned back to Dougal as the old man added, 'The boy thinks ah'm awa in the heid.' He tapped his forehead for emphasis and gave a wink. 'Ah wouldnae hae missed this fer the world.'

'I think he could well be right,' Reverend Shackleford retorted with a sigh, abandoning all attempts to reassure Dougal that they had his best interests at heart. 'You and I both know you'd relish the opportunity to cause an international incident.'

The old Scot laughed delightedly and slapped his thigh. 'Aye, ye be a sight fer sore eyes, Augustus,' he declared. 'Ah've truly missed yer wit.' He looked back to Rosie. 'An it's nae often ah'm gaen the opportunity tae hae a bonny lass on ma arm. Where ye be takin' me the morra, then?'

Rosie looked uncertainly at her grandfather. 'We thought we'd show you the village of Blackmore,' she smiled. 'Then I will leave you in my grandfather's hands while he takes you for lunch in the Red Lion.' She gave a small cough before adding, 'And in the afternoon, we thought you might like to see a little of the Devonshire countryside. The Duke has been kind enough to allow us the use of his carriage.'

'Will yer wife, Agnes, be comin' along wi' us, Augustus? Ah've nae haed a chance tae meet wi' her yet.'

Roseanna looked around, suddenly realising that her step grandmother wasn't present. Even she knew it was very unlike Agnes to miss a free meal. 'I thought grandmama would be here this evening,' she stated. 'Is she unwell perchance?'

'One of her megrims,' the Reverend answered, 'though I suspect this month's periodical might have arrived a day early. Mrs Higgins sent her a full dinner.' Rosie fought the urge to grin. Her grandmother never went anywhere without her salts, regularly swooning at even the slightest upset. Indeed, every house with a Shackleford residing in it was furnished with at least one chaise longue. The histrionics never seemed to affect Agnes's appetite though.

'Well, please give her my love and tell her if she is well enough, I would welcome her company in the carriage tomorrow.'

Her grandfather gave a snort. 'I'll ask her, but If it's between the hours of two and four, you'd have more chance of becoming leg shackled to the King of England than getting her off that deuced chaise.' He turned to Dougal, who was listening to their discussion, his eyes bright with interest. 'I'm certain Agnes…' but what he was certain of was interrupted as Mrs Tenner stepped into the room and banged a small gong.

'Your graces, dinner is served,' she intoned with an imperious bend of her head.

Unfortunately, the stampede of youngsters that followed her announcement was anything but well-mannered.

Predictably, Dougal was seated between Roseanna and the Reverend at dinner and despite her anxiety at the thought of spending the next few days in the company of the irascible old Scot, Rosie found herself actually enjoying his company. Surprisingly, her grandfather too was in fine form, and the time passed more quickly than she'd expected.

As the dinner was drawing to a close and the younger family members taken off to bed, she suddenly wondered how on earth the Duke was going to get his brothers-in-law alone. If Dougal got wind of what was happening behind the scenes, everything would go to hell in a handcart. Despite having known him for only a few hours, Rosie fully accepted that the universally expressed concerns had definitely not been overstated.

But she needn't have worried. The Duke's manner indicated that any private conversation would undoubtedly take place after the rest of the family was abed. A few minutes later, the ladies rose to leave the gentlemen to their port. As she got to her feet, Rosie gave her grandfather a questioning look, unfortunately intercepted by Dougal, who gave a dark chuckle.

'Dinnae fash yersel, lass,' he grinned. 'Ah'll nae be giein yer grandda any flumgummery this night. A wee whisky an' ah'll be ready fer ma bed.'

Indeed, Dougal was as good as his word, and after bidding everyone goodnight along with a bow that would have impressed Brummel himself, he disappeared up the stairs. The Reverend too didn't linger, and Rosie was reminded that despite his larger-than-life character, her grandfather was no spring chicken. As she watched the Duchess order a carriage to be brought round, Rosie couldn't help but notice the slight concern in her aunt's eyes as she kissed her father goodnight.

Glancing over at the large grandfather clock, Rosie allowed herself to think about her upcoming assignation with Tristan Bernart for the first time that evening. The footman had not been waiting on the table during dinner, so for the most part, she'd been able to push it out of her mind. She'd told no one of her intention - not even Francesca. In truth, she'd felt particularly uncomfortable keeping such a secret from her sister - usually, she and Frankie told each other absolutely everything. Picking anxiously at her skirt, Roseanna told herself that this was different. She was not meeting the footman for a romantic tryst, and her uncle had made it clear earlier that the discussion in the study was not to go beyond those four walls. But it still felt to Rosie like a betrayal. And not only that, she was entirely certain that her uncle's edict most definitely precluded any clandestine meetings in the dark.

Watching her cousins play charades, Roseanna wondered if she should simply decide not to go. Certainly, it would be the sensible option, but in her heart of hearts, she knew that wild horses wouldn't keep her away. And that was the most troubling thing of all.

∽

By the time Tristan had finished his chores, it was nearly time for his meeting with Lady Roseanna. In truth, he couldn't imagine what had come over him to arrange such an encounter – and with a young woman of noble birth with whom he'd conversed on only three occasions. What was even more surprising was her acceptance. He told himself he was merely looking out for her welfare and simply wished to warn her against anything foolish. But what could be more foolish than meeting a strange man in the garden at night? Truly, he was bloody addled.

He didn't know what it was about her that drew him. While he was no stranger to women, he'd certainly never felt this unaccountable urge to protect one before. While he was incarcerated in Mont St. Michel, Tristan had spent months without uttering a word and since then, conversation had never come easy to him. Indeed, most of the time, the whole idea of talking for talking's sake was completely foreign to him – even after he'd become fluent in English.

While he was at school, he'd spent most of his time alone. Friendships were something to be wary of, and he was most comfortable in his own company. It wasn't that he was considered rude – though the Duke's niece might well disagree – and he was mostly liked well enough by his peers. They just considered him odd – but then, odd was to be expected from a *frog*. The term was mostly used in jest, and in truth, Tristan felt no loyalty to his former countrymen. They'd nearly killed him after all.

The only loyalty he had was to Roan Carew. Without his mentor, Tristan had no doubt he would not have survived into adulthood. Likely he would have starved to death in that hellhole, but even after escaping – it was Roan who gave him a reason to keep living.

Inevitably, his thoughts drifted back to the mystery of Etienne Babin and the Comte d'Ansouis. He did not think the bogus Count would recognise him. The scrawny lad he'd been while he was at Babin's mercy had long since gone. As had his French accent – though he could still speak his birth country's language well enough.

He didn't dare examine his feelings about the brute who'd abused him so much – those emotions had been firmly locked away in a remote corner of his mind. Nevertheless, he didn't doubt that Babin had killed his saviour. Their subsequent discovery about the *Revisionists* could well provide the key as to why.

Taking off his apron, he glanced over at old Mrs Higgins, asleep in her customary chair next to the range, before speaking in a low voice to the other two servants still finishing off the dishes. Unusually, the rest of the kitchen staff were already abed. They'd been given leave to retire early in preparation for the long gruelling hours they'd be working once the guests began arriving for the annual party.

Bidding the kitchen boy and maid a good night, he picked up a candleholder. The candle in its cradle was already burned halfway down, but with luck, it would last another hour or so. Holding it high, he made his way towards the door leading out into the kitchen garden, but before opening it, he placed the small light on a shelf set high in the wall. He guessed that Roseanna would likely come this way, and he would not have her stumble in the dark. Lifting the latch, he gave a dark, twisted smile. What a considerate man he was... The irony of it had him gritting his teeth.

Unfortunately, the feeling that he was behaving like a craven rogue didn't leave him as he stepped out into the night and he held the door open, fighting the sense of shame that swamped him. It didn't matter that he had no intention of taking advantage of a young, innocent woman. The meeting alone was enough to ruin her. He hesitated in the doorway. The whole thing was pure madness. But there was still time to cry off.

Suddenly certain, he turned to go back inside, only to see the shadowed shape of a lady walking towards him, a little dog at her heels.

∼

Trembling, Roseanna clipped on Trixie's lead and picked up her shawl. She'd retired early as usual and could only hope that no one came to check on her before they retired. Just in case, she placed one of the pillows vertically under the bedclothes. Without a light, anybody looking would think her asleep. Then, picking the little dog up, she moved towards the door. Her heart was thudding hard against her ribs as the sheer folly of what she was doing consumed her mind. Gnawing anxiously at her bottom lip, she pushed the door open a little way and peeked out onto the landing. It was empty. Breathing a sigh of relief, she stepped out and put Trixie down onto the floor. If anyone should stop her, she was simply taking the dog out to do her business. It was certainly not an untruth, though her inability to lie would undoubtedly see her in the suds.

To her relief, she met no one, and within five minutes of leaving her bedchamber, she entered the seldom used corridor leading to the kitchen garden. Fortunately, a lone candle had been left on a shelf, so she was able to see her way. Seconds later, she slowed, almost to a halt as she realised there was a figure standing in the doorway at the end of the corridor. Despite the shadows, she knew instantly that the person holding the door open was the man she was coming to meet.

# Twelve

Trixie gave a soft, warning growl, and flustered, Roseanna bent to pick her up. Then, swallowing nervously, she increased her pace until she was mere feet away. To her consternation, Tristan neither spoke nor moved, but simply stared at her, unsmiling.

'What did you wish to speak to me about?' she asked, not knowing what else to say. In answer, he closed his eyes briefly and bent his head. Was he about to send her away? Unexpectedly, Rosie felt sheer panic swamp her. She somehow knew that if he sent her away now, the two of them would never again be alone together.

Then she almost gasped out loud with the realisation that she actually *wanted* this. This, *and so much more.*

Holding the little dog to her, she took a hesitant step forward and his head snapped up, his eyes now glittering in the candlelight. 'I need to take Trixie outside,' she whispered. For a second, he didn't move, then with a faint sigh that almost sounded like a groan, he opened the door wider and stepped aside.

Swallowing again, Rosie slipped past him and continued towards the kitchen garden without looking back. Her heart was slamming against her chest as though she'd been running. As she put Trixie on to the ground, and unclipped the lead, there was silence behind her. Had he gone back inside?

Then, seconds later, she heard the sound of footsteps approaching and almost sobbed in relief. 'You shouldn't be here.' The voice, when it came, was low, anguished - and so close, she could feel the heat from his body against her back.

'It's a little late for that now,' she responded shakily, determinedly watching the little dog as she nosed along the path.

His silence spoke volumes, but he didn't step back, and she closed her eyes, imagining the feel of his lips against her neck. Dear Lord, what on earth was wrong with her?

'What the devil have you done to me?' he breathed, almost echoing her thoughts.

Unaccountably, Roseanna felt her breasts tighten, the nipples hardened to points at his heated whisper. A slam of sensation caused a liquid heat at the juncture of her thighs and underneath her heavy skirts, she clamped her legs together, fighting the sudden urge to twist round and press herself against him.

Swallowing, she struggled to get her raging emotions under control. She'd been introduced to several eligible gentlemen, but none had left her with even the slightest urge to throw herself into their arms. She clenched her nails into her palms, her breath coming out in short pants, as she tried to rid her body of the unwelcome sensations.

Of course, the principal problem was that Roseanna was deceiving herself. The sensations might have been unexpected, but they weren't unwelcome. Not even a little bit.

'What did you want to speak with me about?' she managed to repeat eventually, her voice a hoarse whisper. Truly, she felt as though there was an invisible string, dragging her backwards towards his heat.

His indrawn breath was the only sign that he'd heard her question, but moments later, he finally stepped back, leaving Rosie with the abrupt feeling that she'd lost something precious.

Shivering, she forced herself to turn round until she faced him. Even though he was now standing a good two feet away, she could sense the tenseness radiating from his body.

In the dim light, she couldn't see the expression in his eyes, but his voice, when he eventually spoke, was impassive. She had no idea how much it cost him.

'I don't wish to see you hurt,' he stated. 'Make no mistake, the man who calls himself Pierre d'Ansouis is a dangerous man. At the very least, he has no morals. I do not yet know his motives, but I *do* know he will kill to protect himself and his secrets. From the information you overheard, we cannot discount the possibility that he already has something afoot.'

'My uncle has made it clear that I am not to involve myself in anything other than Dougal Galbraith's amusement.' She grimaced, well aware that the coming weekend was going to be challenging, even without the inclusion of a possible murder conspiracy. 'The rest I will gladly leave to you.'

Tristan stared at her for a second before nodding his head. 'If something untoward happens – *anything* – promise you will tell me.' His voice was low but fervent, and Roseanna suddenly realised that he truly was concerned for her safety. This hadn't all been an elaborate ruse to get her alone...

She became aware that he was waiting for her answer, and she gave him a swift nod. 'If I hear anything at all, I promise I will get word to you.' She meant it too. Though she knew her family would move heaven and earth to protect her, she also realised there was too much at stake for any of them to focus attention on the possible imaginings of a young woman with a fertile imagination.

'I have to go.' The words sent a shard of ice through Rosie's heart. She took a deep breath, quashing the urge to protest. They'd not had nearly enough time together.

'When can we meet again?' The words came out unbidden, and she could have bitten out her tongue.

Tristan didn't answer at once, but even in the darkness, she could see his jaw tense as he gritted his teeth. Did he want rid of her?

'I have to meet with your father and uncles,' he answered tersely at length. 'D'Ansouis will arrive tomorrow, and the other guests - including Wellington and Grey, the day after. We cannot afford to take any chances.'

Roseanna bit her lip and nodded her head. He was making her no empty promises. His role was to fool d'Ansouis and infiltrate the Revisionists. Given what she'd overheard in the library, his success could well mean the difference between life and death.

This meeting had been foolhardy in the extreme – on both their parts. But she held on to the knowledge that he felt *something* for her, and once it was all over… She reigned in her thoughts. Now was not the time.

'Go,' she murmured, fighting a sudden urge to cry. Then, squaring her shoulders, she turned back to watch for Trixie. She may have been gone from her bedchamber for less than twenty minutes, but in that time, her life had changed irrevocably. When all this was over, she was determined that Tristan Bernart would not escape her so easily.

But that meant keeping him alive in the meantime.

∼

Nicholas's brothers-in-law did not hide their frustration at being kept in the dark about the Comte d'Ansouis. Adam especially favoured him with such a flat, stony stare that the Duke wondered for one horrible moment whether he'd be forced to name his seconds. Of course, Nicholas knew well that the Earl was simply furious that such a deadly secret had been kept from him by the man he considered his closest friend. The others, too, expressed varying degrees of anger and did not hesitate to voice their opinions. Even though Roan and Jamie had also been privy to the plan, it was Nicholas who received the brunt of their annoyance. Unfairly, Nicholas thought privately.

Still, he bore the censure stoically without retaliating and allowed them to have their say. And, when they'd finally finished their combined diatribe, Nicholas asked for their help.

To be fair, once the men had properly voiced their resentment, they all offered their assistance with commendable enthusiasm and by three a.m., they'd come up with a strategy Nicholas hoped would work.

~

By the time Rosie woke the next morning, the time she'd spent with Tristan felt like some fantastical dream. Staring up at the counterpane above her bed, she went over their whole meeting again. Had she made a complete cake of herself? Mayhap she'd imagined the longing in his whispered words. The small voice in her head persisted in going over and over every second of their time in the garden, but there was never any simple conclusion.

In truth, she knew that now was not the time to be casting lovesick eyes towards anyone, let alone a pretend footman. Despite the intensity of the short time they'd spent together, she still knew almost nothing about Tristan - who he was really and how he'd come to be involved in the conspiracy. From the things they'd let slip whilst in the study, she understood he had a connection to her Uncle Roan. But what it was exactly, she still had no idea.

And tempted as she was to ask her cousin Henrietta, Rosie realised that even suggesting the possibility that one of Blackmore's servants had some kind of secret connection to her father would likely create a whole new set of problems. No, for the time being, her role was to keep Dougal Galbraith away from the whole smoky business.

~

'Thunder an' turf, what the deuce is that you're eating?' Reverend Shackleford stared in horrified fascination at the unidentifiable lump of *something* that Dougal was chewing on.

'Ah dinnae ken tae be honest. It tastes a bit like ma old da's boots.' Dougal eyed the lump in his hand, then shrugged and bit off another piece.

'I really don't think you should be eating that, Mr Galbraith,' Roseanna advised with a wince. 'I actually think it might have been left by one of the dogs.'

'I'm not even going to ask how you know what your father's boots tasted like,' the Reverend muttered. 'For pity's sake, man, throw it away.'

Dougal grinned, took another bite and threw the offending piece of whatever it was over the side of the barouche. Only Roseanna's quick reflexes prevented Trixie from launching herself after it. Flossy, on the other hand, didn't bother to move, having far more experience when it came to unidentifiable edible objects.

They'd left Blackmore twenty minutes earlier in the Duke's brand-new, up-to-the-minute barouche. It was wonderfully comfortable, and the open top meant that passengers could take in the surroundings as they passed. Rosie had never really had a tour of the vast estate that comprised the Duke's country seat, and she was enjoying it immensely. She'd had no idea quite how big the Blackmore estate actually was – it entirely dwarfed her father's estate at Northwood.

As they bowled through the parkland, she caught sight of a herd of deer. When she was younger, Rosie remembered crying after catching sight of a deer carcass after the gentlemen returned from a hunt. Her uncle had not dismissed her tears as histrionics and had taken the time to carefully explain that if the herd was left to get too large, it could cause a great deal of damage to the environment. It was the only time he allowed hunting on Blackmore land.

Rosie also knew that after culling, unless the animal was diseased, the resulting meat was shared with the villagers, which helped to discourage poachers.

'How is grandmama this morning?' Rosie asked her grandfather after the herd disappeared from view.

'She was still abed when I left,' the Reverend answered. 'She likes to take her *physic* an hour before breakfast.'

'What exactly is in it?' Roseanna asked curiously.

'I have no idea,' the Reverend sighed, giving a small shudder. 'In truth, I dread to think. Foul stuff it is.' He paused, then gave a small chuckle. 'I remember once, before your Aunt Grace married the Duke, she attracted the interest of a young teacher…'

'Was he handsome?' Rosie interrupted, interested.

'What does that have to do with anything?' the Reverend retorted.

'De ye nae ken, Augustus? A lad may be a tumshie heid as long as he haes a pretty face.'

The Reverend sat thinking for a second. 'If by *tumshie heid* you mean dull-witted, I can only say that on this occasion, Mr Carruthers was possessed of neither intelligence nor looks. As I recall, he was particularly overweight with a face full of pimples.'

Rosie gave a shudder. 'He sounds dreadful. How on earth could you have considered him for Aunt Grace?'

'I'd have considered the devil himself back then if old Nick had come courting. Suitors for a hoydenish bookworm who spoke her mind at the most inconvenient moments were not exactly ten-a-penny.'

Roseanna blinked. She knew her Aunt Grace was not the most conventional Duchess, but it was hard to imagine her as a wild outspoken young woman – especially being married to a stern man like Nicholas Sinclair. 'So, what happened?' she asked, intrigued.

'Well, as you can imagine, the vicarage was full to bursting with bickering females,' her grandfather answered with a small grimace. 'It was enough to make a grown man weep. Young Mr Carruthers fancied himself as South Devonshire's Lord Byron.' He snorted, shaking his head. 'The truth was, he was a pompous bore, and Grace would have none of him. Agnes thought it a good match and invited the fellow for dinner.' He paused and looked into the distance, lost for a second in his memories. 'It was around the time Percy arrived, if I remember rightly.' He looked at Roseanna with a sudden grin. 'When I introduced 'em, Grace thought *he* was a suitor and deuced well swooned – went straight to the floor.'

Rosie tried to imagine the spindle-legged, balding curate as a young man and failed.

'Anyway,' the Reverend went on, 'Mr Carruthers came for dinner, but unbeknown to me, the girls had pilfered Agnes's physic – though they never admitted which of 'em did the deed. One of the chits laced the poor fellow's pudding with the stuff. I reckon they must have used the whole deuced bottle because the bum brusher spent the entire night on the privy.'

Though it was unseemly to find humour in another man's misfortune, Roseanna couldn't help giggling, while Dougal slapped his leg and guffawed.

'So, the tumshie haed the back door trots? I'll wager ye nivver seen him agin.'

'Agnes was up in the boughs for weeks. Said she'd never be able to show her face in church again. Fortunately, the Duke of Blackmore happened to be looking for a bride not long after that, so all's well that ends well...' The Reverend paused and sighed before adding, 'Though it has to be said, Grace made a mull of that in the beginning.'

'Really?' Both Dougal and Rosie leaned forward, the scenery completely forgotten. At the sight of their identical captivated expressions, Augustus Shackleford caught himself. Tare an' hounds, what the devil was he doing indulging in such prittle prattle? He could almost feel the Almighty glaring down at him.

He leaned back with a self-conscious cough, before muttering, 'Well, naturally, you'll have to ask the Duchess herself about that…'

## Thirteen

Tristan had spent the entire night tossing and turning - so much so that the two other footmen sharing the chamber each put their pillow over their head in an effort to block out the noise of his fidgeting. Tris suspected he'd been lucky they hadn't used the pillows to smother him instead.

What madness had come over him the night before? And dear God, he'd almost kissed her. Tristan groaned. The picture that came with the thought of his lips plundering such feminine softness produced an instant hardness.

Thankful he was alone in the dining room, Tristan took off his white glove and adjusted himself, trying to ease the tightness of his breeches. He could only hope she didn't decide to share details of their tryst with… Devil take it, he didn't even know whose daughter she was. Only that her name was Roseanna. The whole thing was utter madness.

Groaning, he replaced the glove and determinedly continued laying the table, forcing his traitorous mind back to the matter at hand. Dinner tonight would be more formal with the arrival of the Comte, but it would still be a small affair compared to the fifty plus people who would be seated at the table over the weekend.

The Comte was due to arrive early afternoon and Tristan knew that today was his best chance to attract d'Ansouis's attention given that from tomorrow the house would be filled to bursting. It was hard to call the nobleman by that name, knowing that the real Count had likely been put to bed with a spade. But he didn't dare refer to the murdering bastard as *Babin* – even in his head. It could so easily slip out.

The Duke had been informed that the Comte would not be bringing his own valet, so from the time of his arrival, Tristan would act as such. That would hopefully give them enough time together to sow the necessary seeds. However, once the other guests arrived, there would be little time for small talk in the bedchamber. And, if the *Revisionists'* leader *was* planning something...

Tristan felt his gut clench. Truly, the stakes could not be higher, and the next twenty-four hours were crucial. He could ill afford *any* distractions. So, whatever it was he felt for Roseanna would simply have to be pushed deep down, and in time he'd forget...

∽

'So, Augustus, this be yer local tavern? Dae they hae a decent whisky?'

The Reverend frowned as he led Dougal to his and Percy's customary table. 'I'm not sure there's much of a call for it, but they have a very passable local ale.' Thankfully, the inn was empty but for the two of them. Clearly, most of the villagers were out in the fields, preparing for the coming harvest.

The Scot shrugged and sat down, looking around him with interest.

'What can I get yer, Revren.' The landlady's voice echoed in the empty bar.

'Noo, *that* be a handsome lass,' Dougal commented, admiring the buxom matron behind the bar. 'Whit be her name?'

'Her name's Mary, but you can put your deuced tongue away,' Augustus Shackleford growled. 'The lady's only recently widowed and wouldn't be interested in an old rascal like you.'

Dougal merely grinned at the clergyman and gave a lewd wink. The Reverend's heart sank. This was all he needed, trying to keep the old goat away from Percy's mother as well as the man's adopted son. He sighed before looking heavenward and murmuring, 'Point taken.'

Not wanting to give his companion any more encouragement, the Reverend quickly made his way to the bar. 'How are you, Mary?' he asked, particularly mindful of his duty as God's representative on earth since the Almighty had just all but slapped him on the head with it.

Mary eyed him in surprise. 'I'm keepin' busy,' she answered. 'Percy's bin comin' by every day.'

Reverend Shackleford felt a sudden rush of shame. He'd been so consumed with his own problems, he'd all but lost sight of what was important, and it had taken a less than subtle nudge in the ribs from upstairs to remind him of it.

'That's good,' he answered sheepishly, vowing to call into church straight after dinner and offer his divine employer his humble apologies. 'If there's anything I can do, Mary, you only have to ask.' The landlady gave him a largely toothless smile.

'What can I get yer Revren?' she asked again.

'Two tankards of your best ale, Mary, please, and two of your mutton pies.'

'I'm thinkin' that scrawny cove over there makin' eyes at me is your granddaughter's da-in-law?'

'He is, indeed, madam. Pay him no mind.' The Reverend turned to give Dougal a glare. The old Scot responded with a thumbs up sign.

'Will Percy be joinin' yer both?' Mary asked, sliding two tankards of foaming ale across the bar.

Reverend Shackleford nodded as he picked up the tankards. 'I reckon he'll be here before one.'

'In that case, I'll make up another pie so it's nice an' 'ot when 'e gets 'ere.' Mary wiped her hands on a none too clean rag and disappeared into the back.

'That's Percy's mother you're ogling,' the Reverend hissed when he got back to their table. 'I'll thank you to keep your wandering eyes on your ale.'

Dougal grinned unrepentantly and picked up his tankard. 'Ah dinnae hae any idea whit ye blatherin' on aboot,' he declared, before taking a deep draft and smacking his lips appreciatively. 'Aye ye be right, Augustus - the bonny lass surely ken's hoo tae pull a decent pint o' ale.'

Augustus Shackleford gritted his teeth. The mutton head must be deuced short sighted. Mary had been called many things over the years, but a bonny lass was not one of them.

'Hoo's the lad settlin' in?' Dougal asked, laying his tankard back on the table. 'Whit were 'is name?' He thought for a second. 'Finn, aye that be it. Ma heart gaes oot tae the poor bugger livin' wi' all these bloody sassenachs.'

Reverend Shackleford's heart stuttered at the Scot's mention of Finn, but he rallied quickly and managed, 'Finn's settled in very nicely. He's a grand boy. Very bright. Loves school.'

'He be learnin' his letters?' Dougal's surprise was genuine.

The Reverend gave an enthusiastic nod. 'Oh yes, Finn loves school. In fact, he spends hardly any time at home.' The clergyman was determined to nip any suggestion of Dougal seeing the boy right in the bud. 'Why Percy was only saying the other day just how much the boy enjoys his learning. Indeed, the school master described the lad as his best pupil. Finn is very conscientious. Not at all like most boys...' Catching sight of Dougal's disbelieving face, the Reverend trailed off, and gave another vigorous nod for good measure. He took a sip of his ale, wondering if he'd done it a bit too brown.

Dougal opened his mouth to speak but was distracted by Mary coming back into the bar. 'The pies are in an' won't be long. I've some pickled eggs if you fancy while yer waitin' gentlemen.'

'Ooh, ah'll hae one,' a small voice piped up from the door. 'Ma belly's thinkin' ma heid's bin chopped off. Ah be starvin.'

The Reverend spluttered into his pint. '*Tare an' hounds*. Shouldn't you be in school, Finn Noon?' he thundered, hoping to scare the lad into beating a hasty retreat.

Instead, Finn grinned over at him. 'Nae, Revren. Maister Smith sent me oot fer giein' Willie a black eye. An' ye ken ah hate school. Is this the auld bampot ye've tae keep oot o' mischief?' He eyed Dougal with interest before adding, 'Well dinnae fash yersel, yer Revrenship. Ah be here tae help.'

While the Reverend and Dougal were out to lunch at the Red Lion, Roseanna asked John, their barouche driver, to set her down at the gates to Blackmore. Walking back to the house would give both her and Trixie some exercise, not to mention reduce the amount of time she was required to be sociable during the informal lunch being served in the small dining room. Naturally, she wanted to spend *some* time with her sister and cousins – just not too much. She knew too that her mother and father would be wishing to speak with her at some point. Her decision to help her grandfather look after Dougal Galbraith instead of mixing with potential suitors would, Rosie knew, disappoint her mama especially.

Letting Trixie off her lead, Roseanna strolled along the path that had been laid parallel to the long drive. Trees and flowering shrubs along the route made for a very pleasant perambulation, but being deep in thought, Rosie hardly took note of the picturesque surrounds.

She knew well that her mother worried about her. For women in their situation, the options were either marriage or spinsterhood, and either course meant being dependent on others for even the most basic needs. Roseanna knew she was incredibly lucky to have parents who were tolerant of her foibles. They loved her dearly. But that didn't mean she would ultimately have the luxury of forging her own path – especially since she still had no idea what that path was.

She knew that she wanted to be married - but to a man who respected her, at the very least. Not an autocratic tyrant who believed her his, to do with as he wished. And there lay the rub. The law stated that once a woman married, she, and everything she owned, became the property of her husband. So, as Rosie saw it, making sure to choose the *right* man for a husband was imperative. Kindness, patience and tolerance were the qualities most important to her. But more than that, she dearly wished for her husband to actually *like* her.

But, at the end of the day, she might have a bit of an odd kick in her gallop, as her grandfather was fond of saying, but she wasn't stupid. Rosie knew that one day reasonably soon she would have to wed. So far, her mother and father had respected her reluctance to play the marriage mart with a season in London. Indeed, Francesca too was balking at the idea. Jennifer and Mercedes had both declared it tedious in the extreme, and neither had found their husbands as a result of it. So too her aunts. Not one had taken part in a season and come away with a husband – certainly not in the conventional sense anyway. But then, country vicars' daughters weren't traditionally considered *ton* material.

Deep in thought, Rosie paid little heed to her surroundings until she rounded the bend, and the magnificence of Blackmore came suddenly into view. Pausing, she stared in awe at the glorious house that was the centre of the Duke of Blackmore's seat. Truly, it was a sight to behold. Her own home of Northwood paled in comparison. She'd visited so often throughout her childhood, but had never really *looked* at it before. What were the odds of her future husband being the master of something like this?

Shaking her head, she started walking again. She couldn't even begin to imagine being the chatelaine of such a place. Indeed, she had no idea how her Aunt Grace did it. Especially since the Duchess had apparently once thought nothing of tying her garter in public - if the story her grandfather had related earlier was to be believed.

But then, not all of her family were married into old aristocratic families. She'd been told her Uncle Roan had grown up on the streets of Torquay until being press-ganged into the Royal Navy. Uncle Jago was the owner of a tin mine in Cornwall, and Uncle Jamie was a local boy – born and brought up in Blackmore.

And now Jennifer, the daughter of a Duke, had married a penniless steward…

Roseanna finally allowed herself to think about Tristan Bernart. In truth, all her musings to now had determinedly avoided any thoughts of the handsome Frenchman.

Her face heated as she thought back to the evening before. He'd wanted to kiss her – and more. She might be naïve, perhaps even a little unclear of what *more* might involve, but she recognised her body's response to his nearness. The way her heart spiked, and the triangle between her legs thrummed with guilty pleasure. His breath on the back of her neck had even caused her breasts to tingle and her nipples to harden. It was all very new and exciting. But what did he really feel for her? Was it lust or something more? She wasn't sure she quite understood the difference.

In their dealings, he certainly hadn't come across as either kind or patient. And she'd never seen any indication that he actually liked her. Indeed, if asked, she would have said it was exactly the opposite. In all honesty, she knew nothing about him, but from what she'd seen, he was everything she *didn't* want in a man.

So why did he consume her thoughts so?

# Fourteen

It wasn't often that Augustus Shackleford was truly frustrated with the Almighty. Experience had shown that it never did any good, though there was the odd occasion he felt the need to have more than a quiet word.

This was one of those occasions.

Indeed, as Finn plonked himself down on the chair next to Dougal, pickled egg in his grubby hand, the Reverend found himself not only frustrated, but, if truth be told, a little disheartened. He'd always prided himself on being attuned to the moods of his maker, but in this instance, there was a strong possibility he'd got it entirely wrong.

He glowered at the lad, who was now in the process of dropping bits of yolk down the front of his equally grubby smock.

'Hoo be things in Caerlaverock?' Finn was asking the old Scot. 'Ah cannae wait tae see the Lady Jennifer.'

'Aye, ah'm certain she be o' the same mind laddie.' Dougal gave a largely toothless grin just as the door opened to admit Percy.

'Da, look who be here?' Fin yelled excitedly. 'An' ma heid hasnae bin turned once, honest.' He swivelled in his chair to give the Reverend a reassuring thumbs up, only for his smile to falter as he caught sight of the clergyman's sour face.

'Be somethin' wrong wi' ye, Revren?' Finn quizzed him, uncertainly.

At the sight of the young lad's distress, Augustus Shackleford felt his ire disappear. His earlier internal monologue popped abruptly back into his head, promptly followed by the proverb, *pride comes before a fall*. He nearly laughed out loud. Tare an' hounds, the Almighty was merely reminding him that he was a deuced pudding head. This lad was someone special. That's all he needed to know.

'A touch of gout, lad, is all.' He ruffled the boy's hair and added gruffly, 'If your da gives his permission, Lady Roseanna and I are taking Mr Galbraith for a jaunt in the Duke's barouche as soon as we've eaten. Would you like to come with us?'

Finn's shining eyes were his reward.

Percy raised his eyebrows as he sat down. Obviously, he had no idea what had brought about Reverend Shackleford's sudden change of heart, and as always, the curate's immediate thought was that his superior was up to something. Sending Finn off to who knew where with only the impetuous clergyman to supervise him was a recipe for disaster - and the fact that even the Reverend himself considered Dougal Galbraith to be a totty-headed menace, did not bode well.

However, the last thing Percy wanted to do was disappoint the boy, and the incident with Willie notwithstanding, Finn had been working hard on his letters, and in his adopted father's opinion, deserved a reward. And truly, the curate was confident that nothing untoward was likely to happen in only a pair of hours.

After a few seconds, Percy sighed and said, 'I think that's a splendid idea. In actual fact, I have some free time this afternoon. Why don't I come along too?'

Augustus Shackleford looked at his curate in astonishment. As far as he could remember, this was the first time Percy had ever actually invited himself on a caper – innocent or otherwise. Indeed, the Reverend found himself suddenly blinking back tears. After their escapade in the London Docks, not two months earlier, the clergyman had firmly believed that his curate had participated in his last ever havey cavey affair. But, despite being as chuckle-headed as ever, it appeared that Percy was yet willing to throw himself into another adventure. It was enough to make a grown man weep.

Of course, what Reverend Shackleford had forgotten, being a man of advancing years, was that Percy Noon actually knew nothing of what was currently happening at Blackmore and had merely agreed to a pleasant afternoon drive. The curate was therefore even less equipped than usual to deal with the potentially deadly turn of events that unfolded over the following few hours.

∽

Before heading to the informal luncheon, Roseanna took Trixie back to her bedchamber. The little dog was perfectly content to snooze on the bed, having covered at least twice the distance of her mistress on their walk up from the gatehouse.

An unsigned note had been left for her stating that the Comte d'Ansouis was expected to arrive early evening and had already requested that his evening meal be served in his bedchamber, citing a desire to be fresh for the entertainments beginning the following day. She couldn't help breathing a sigh of relief since it meant that she and her grandfather would not have to watch Dougal like hawks during dinner. Ripping the note into tiny pieces to prevent anyone else reading it and wondering why Lady Roseanna Atwood was being informed of the Comte d'Ansouis' plans, she wrapped the pieces into an old kerchief and stuffed them into the bottom of a drawer. Then, after quickly freshening up in the bowl of rosewater left on her dressing table, Rosie made her way downstairs to join the rest of the family.

The atmosphere over lunch was decidedly subdued. Indeed, so much so that those members of the family not privy to the disaster they were teetering on were left a trifle bewildered.

Being aware of the reason behind the sober mood conversely prompted Roseanna to be at her most vivacious, which further bemused both her sister and her cousins, not to mention her mother who was looking at her as though she'd sprouted two heads. Fortunately, much to Rosie's relief, her father wasn't present to query her sudden vivacity, and neither was she discomfited by the presence of Tristan Bernart serving at the table.

Indeed, she suspected that both men were closeted in the Duke's study with the other missing male members of the family.

'Ah dae hope ma father's behaving himself, Lady Roseanna, an' ah'd just like tae thank ye fer volunteering tae help look after him.'

Roseanna looked over at Brendon Galbraith and smiled. Thankfully, Jennifer's handsome husband was nothing like his father at all. 'It's really no bother,' she responded, smiling. 'Both Grandpapa and I thoroughly enjoyed showing Mr Galbraith around the Blackmore estate this morning.' As she spoke, Rosie was surprised to discover that she wasn't exaggerating – she actually had enjoyed herself. 'I have to admit that seeing it from a newcomer's perspective has opened my eyes somewhat. I had no idea it was so big.'

Brendon chuckled. 'Ah can guess ma da had a few choice words tae say aboot it.'

'My grandfather was telling us about life in the vicarage whilst my aunts were growing up, and I suspect Mr Galbraith enjoyed hearing about it as much as I did. I had no idea that my mother and aunts had such an enthralling childhood.'

Overhearing their conversation, her Aunt Patience gave an inelegant snort. 'I don't think any of us would have described it as *enthralling*. Unconventional, most definitely. For the most part, Father simply left us to our own devices, so we basically did whatever we wanted.'

'What happened in the vicarage, remains in the vicarage,' Charity interrupted, laughing.

And, just like that, the sombre mood dissipated as her mother and aunts began reminiscing.

'Do you remember when Anthony fell into the pond at Wistman's Wood and Pru told him he'd turn into a ghoul?' Chastity favoured her brother with a wide grin. 'He thought she meant a bowl of porridge.'

'It's a wonder I survived to adulthood.' Anthony sighed in mock indignation.

'It was while your father was hiding out in Pear Tree cottage,' Faith told Roseanna.

'It was your wedding that Queen Charlotte attended, wasn't it Aunt Hope?' Jennifer wasn't the only one who leaned forward to listen.

'She did, and I hated it,' Hope responded with a sigh. 'Everybody spent the day walking on eggshells until she'd gone.'

'I know something happened, but Grandpapa would never say what.' Jennifer's tone of voice was hopeful, but resigned.

'He never told any of us either.' Prudence laughed. 'But whatever it was, was bad enough that your Aunt Patience had her come out in Bath rather than London.'

'I think we were all grateful for that,' Temperance commented with a grin.

'Speak for yourself,' Patience retorted. 'I never wished to wed in the first place. It was you and Grace who bullied me into it.'

'I shudder even now when I think of what could have happened.' Temperance shook her head, lost for a second in her memories.

'Didn't you want to marry Papa?' Max was frowning, and his mother broke into a peal of laughter.

'Of course I did, darling,' Patience reassured him. 'And in truth, I think your father's probably the only one who would have me.'

'There's no *probably* about it.' Grace commented with a chuckle. 'And I don't think *anybody* will ever be able to fathom how you managed to snare a handsome marquess.'

'I'm a legend,' Patience retorted with a wink as she helped herself to an apple. Then, climbing to her feet, she added, 'Who's for a game of croquet?'

Roseanna couldn't help thinking that her Aunt's abrupt ending of the conversation was deliberate, and she wondered how many more garters her aunts had tied in public.

Uncommonly sad that the lunch had come to an end, she looked down at her pocket watch. She just had time to collect Trixie before leaving to meet her grandfather and Dougal outside the Red Lion. She suspected that John would already be waiting for her in the barouche.

Her intention had been to slip out of the room after giving her mother and sister a swift hug - before they had a chance to ask any questions. Her mother, however, evidently had different ideas. Gripping Rosie's shoulders, Hope stared into her daughter's face. 'Is there anything wrong dearest?' Her question took Roseanna by surprise. She'd thought herself a master at hiding her feelings from the people she loved, but mayhap she wasn't quite as successful as she'd believed.

'I am fine, Mama,' she answered with a smile. 'You have no cause for worry.' Hope gritted her teeth, not believing her daughter's answer for one instant.

'You do not have to do this, Rosie,' she insisted. 'If you wish Nicholas to assign another to Dougal's care, I'm certain he will happily do so. In truth, I think both he and Grace are overreacting about the whole business. I doubt very much that a tactless old man is capable of causing that much trouble. And I'm entirely certain that both Wellington and Grey are accustomed to dealing with much worse.'

Evidently, her father hadn't shared the other, much more perilous, reason for getting Dougal out of the way and she couldn't help wincing internally at the trouble he'd likely find himself in when it was all over, and his wife found out the truth.

Leaning forward, she enfolded her mother in a hug. 'I'm perfectly content to play the nursemaid,' she declared. 'Dougal Galbraith is an interesting character, and of course, Grandpapa is, well… Grandpapa.' She gave an impish grin. 'This morning, I learned about Aunt Grace's suitor – the one you all apparently tried to poison.'

Hope laughed, just as Rosie had hoped. 'Poor Mr Carruthers. I don't think he ever realised what had caused his indisposition.' She returned her daughter's hug before stepping back. 'Make sure you inform me of your return.'

Fortunately, she was not subjected to the same cross-examination from her sister. Frankie had merely demanded her twin reveal all as soon as she returned.

Minutes later, Rosie was hurrying towards the waiting barouche, Trixie under her arm. Breathlessly, she apologised for being late, only to realise, as she did so, that their driver had changed. Her heart sank a little as she realised it was Thomas. He gave her a toothless grin and tipped his cap. She'd first met the one-legged coachman when still only a child. Looking at his grizzled features now, she couldn't even begin to imagine how old he actually was. She just knew that he'd lost his leg in the Battle of Trafalgar and been with the Duke ever since.

As they lurched forward, she gripped the side of the carriage and held tightly onto Trixie. Her Uncle Nicholas had always had a reputation for collecting waifs and strays from his naval days, but she couldn't help but question his decision to employ a coach driver with only one leg. When questioned, her Aunt Grace had laughingly informed her that Thomas had been much worse in his younger days, though, apparently his terrible driving had nothing to do with his missing limb. Unsurprisingly, the Duchess's words hadn't provided much comfort…

∼

Less than twenty minutes later, Thomas brought the barouche to a halt outside the Red Lion. Her grandfather had earlier suggested they take the Totnes Road this afternoon, stopping at a small farmhouse selling scrumpy. Although Rosie had no intention of taking even the smallest sip of the rough, unfiltered apple cider, Dougal had been worryingly enthusiastic. As she waited for the two men to appear, Rosie sighed. While the morning had been entertaining, she wasn't looking forward to the prospect of keeping her companions on the straight and narrow. Even the slightest possibility of either man returning to Blackmore half foxed at the same time as a suspected murdering conspiracist did not bear thinking about.

There was no doubt that this was one of the Reverend's more bacon-brained ideas and Rosie had been sorely tempted to throw a rub in the way. But at the end of the day, she had no wish for her grandfather to end up in the suds.

But then she hadn't realised they'd be accompanied by a one-legged coach driver.

As she waited, her unease gradually increased from a slight feeling of disquiet to a sense of doom reaching almost biblical precautions.

So, when a slight commotion heralded the arrival of her two companions, she was almost hysterically relieved to discover that Percy and Finn would be accompanying them. Their presence would ensure that there was no chance of her grandfather having more than one small cup of cider while his curate was looking on. And then, of course there was Finn.

Rosie wasn't sure what had weakened the Reverend's resolve to keep the lad away from Dougal Galbraith's disruptive influence, but she suspected it might have something to do with Finn's barely restrained excitement at the mere thought of riding in an open top carriage. She moved over so that he and his adoptive father could squeeze in beside her.

'Since there are so many of us, Thomas, I would be grateful if you'd go a little slower. It wouldn't do for any of us to fall out.' Rosie did her best to ensure that her voice contained a pleasing mix of politeness and authority, and overall, she felt satisfied that she had achieved the correct balance.

That was until Thomas flicked the reigns and the horses shot off like they'd been fired from a musket.

# Fifteen

Fortunately, as the barouche left the village, Thomas reined the horses back to a fast trot and Roseanna was finally able to let go of her bonnet.

'Thunder an' turf,' the Reverend muttered, pulling Flossy out from under his cassock. 'What possessed Nicholas to replace John with Thomas?' Assuming it was a rhetorical question, Rosie shook her head and swallowed before letting go of Trixie and retying the strings to her straw bonnet.

'Ah'm thinkin' all Englishmen be awa in the heid,' Dougal grumbled.

'*Thomas*,' Augustus Shackleford roared, 'If you do that again, I'll make sure his grace puts you on grave digging duty. I don't care if you've only got one deuced leg.'

Thomas didn't answer, but the horses slowed down to a sedate trot.

Fortunately, the safest seat had been Finn's since he was wedged in between Rosie and Percy like pilchards in a hogshead. The boy didn't speak, but his expression as the barouche's speed decreased was one of unmistakable disappointment.

Percy didn't move, but after about five minutes he managed to croak, 'I think I'm going to need the privy.'

~

Nicholas stood at the study window, staring out at the incredible vista laid out in front of him. From where he was standing, he could see right down to the lake and the small figures sitting on blankets or paddling in the shallows. The distant shouts and squeals reached him, even through the glass of the window, and the sudden longing for a quiet, simple life was so strong that, without thinking, the Duke laid his head against the glass and closed his eyes.

The weariness felt as though it had settled in his bones. Far worse than anything he'd experienced before. Above everything, Nicholas wanted peace, and in that moment, he made the decision that after this business was done, he would retire from public life. Peter was old enough now to take over much of the reins. In truth, the young man was champing at the bit, and had given his father no reason to doubt either his enthusiasm or competency.

Seating himself in front of the fireplace, Nicholas laid his head against the back of the winged chair. It was past time for him and Grace to slow down. He thought back to their wedding so long ago - to the moment she'd thrown up over his immaculately polished hessians. God's teeth, he'd been a fool back then.

He'd tried so hard to keep her out of his heart. Determined to hold her at arm's length. Why? It seemed nonsensical now, all these years later. He only knew that the day she agreed to wed him was the luckiest day of his life.

A knock at the door interrupted his reverie.

Gritting his teeth, Nicholas lifted his head. 'Come,' he shouted.

Seconds later, the door opened to admit Adam. 'There's no sign of d'Ansouis' carriage,' he declared. 'Prudence is speaking with the servants. She and Jamie have apparently developed an eating disorder which needs to be explained to every servant in the building – with particular emphasis on their background. God knows how Pru comes up with these bizarre ideas.'

Nicholas gave a small chuckle. 'I'm assuming that so far none have displayed a talent for breaking and entering with a side helping of murder. Have you spoken to Temperance?'

Adam shook his head. 'Right now, I think there's a strong possibility I'll never be given the opportunity to speak to her again. When she finds out we've been keeping this from her...' Adam paused and grimaced. 'Truly, this bastard had better turn out to be a murdering lunatic. That's liable to be the only way I'll ever get to sleep in my marriage bed again.'

Nicholas creased his brows, unsure of his best friend's logic. 'So, if he turns out to be completely rational, you'll be relegated to a spare bedchamber?'

'More likely a spare house,' Adam retorted drily. 'You don't happen to have one, do you?'

Nicholas found himself grinning. 'You're as familiar with my holdings as I am. Take your pick. Brandy?'

'I thought you' never ask.' Adam sighed and sat down in the other winged chair.

Climbing to his feet, Nicholas went over to the decanter. 'You're looking tired, my friend,' Adam observed.

'It's been a very trying week,' the Duke retorted, handing Adam a large brandy. 'But the truth is, I'm bone weary.' He sat back down and took a sip of his drink. 'I'm actually thinking of turning more responsibility over to Peter.'

'He's more than capable,' Adam commented. 'And he'll make a fine duke one day.'

Nicholas gave a rueful chuckle. 'The way I'm feeling at the moment, I'm afraid that day may come sooner than he thinks.' Sighing, he pulled an envelope out of his pocket.

'Unfortunately, we have another problem. One that overshadows everything that's happened so far. I received this an hour ago.' He leaned forward and placed the missive into Adam's waiting hand.

The Earl glanced down at the seal and froze. With a soft expletive, he fumbled with the envelope flap, finally managing to tug out the letter it contained. As soon as he finished, he raised incredulous eyes to his oldest friend.

'There's no time to put him off,' Nicholas murmured, his voice oddly philosophical. 'He's already left London and is due here tomorrow.'

Both men sat in disbelieving silence for a few seconds until the Duke added, 'Still, there's always a silver lining to every cloud. We can't deal with this with just the eleven of us. We will have to enlist the aid of the entire family.

'With luck, informing Tempy that the King is coming will take her mind off your sleeping arrangements.'

---

'Tare an' hounds Percy. Can't you just go behind a bush. I can't imagine there's much chance of a privy at the deuced farmhouse anyway – and if there is ... well, a bush might actually be preferable.'

'Ah'd be thankful if ye'd keep a civil tongue in yer head, Augustus. Hae ye forgoat there be a lady present?'

The Reverend hmphed before turning towards his granddaughter. 'My apologies, Rosie. I meant no offense.'

'None taken,' Roseanna responded. 'I actually think there may be a small inn a couple of miles ahead with, err... surprisingly fine facilities.'

'Dae they sell Scrumpy?' Dougal quizzed her.

'I'm afraid I'm unfamiliar with the alcoholic beverages they serve,' Rosie answered primly. 'Truthfully, I have only stopped here once before when we were on the way to Plymouth.'

'Did ye see any ships, milady?' Finn piped up. 'Ah saw lots o' ships in London.'

Rosie smiled at the boy and nodded. 'My father's ship, Cloud Flyer, had returned from the Indies.'

'Did ye gae aboard?' Finn's question was almost breathless, as though he couldn't imagine anything quite so wonderful.

Rosie shook her head. 'Sailors are a very superstitious lot and generally believe that having a woman on board is bad luck, except in very specific circumstances. If you're interested in sailing, why don't you speak with my Uncle Roan. He was a captain in the Royal Navy for quite a few years.'

'As was Nicholas before he became the Duke of Blackmore. His ship was at Trafalgar.'

'What's Trafalgar?' Finn asked. 'Be it somethin' tae dae wi' old Boney? Maister Smith wa' tellin' us aboot the war.'

Percy nodded, forgetting about his bladder for a moment. 'It was at the very beginning. Perhaps I could ask his grace to tell you about when the garden party is over.'

'I'm certain he would oblige,' Reverend Shackleford added, 'though I reckon the memory of it still gives him a few nightmares.'

'Be this the place?' Dougal interrupted, pointing ahead.

Rosie leaned forward and nodded. 'I think so.'

'*Thomas*,' the Reverend yelled, '*pull into the inn yard ahead*.' His muttered, 'Preferably after slowing down,' was confined to his fellow passengers.

A few moments later, they swung into the inn's yard – not quite on two wheels, only narrowly avoiding a waiting carriage.

When they finally came to a halt next to the carriage, the Reverend studied the small painted insignia on the door. 'Well, it looks like there's a nob here, but I don't recognise the crest.' He looked over at the entrance thoughtfully. 'I wonder who it is?'

'Dae ye want me tae go in an' hae a wee peek?' If the Scot was affronted by the chorus of, 'Nos,' he didn't show it.

'If you're going to do your business, you'd best get on with it, Percy,' the Reverend growled. 'At this rate, we won't get back in time for deuced dinner.'

With a relieved nod, the curate hurriedly climbed down, followed closely by Finn. 'Ah'll come wi' ye, Dar, in case ye need protectin'.' The boy's offer was made in all seriousness and his adopted father smiled down at him as they walked towards the entrance, responding with an equally serious, 'Thank you, Finn, that's very kind of you.'

'I think I'll give Trixie a chance to see to her own business,' Rosie said. 'Shall I take Flossy for you?'

'We could hae a wee peek in the bar,' Dougal suggested, 'Ah'll be happy wi' a wee dram instead o' cider.' He gave a sidelong glance towards Rosie. 'More refined fer the lady.'

Rosie bit her lip. The only time she'd ever entered any kind of tavern was with her parents, and then they'd always been shown to a private room. She looked over at the front of the building. Clearly, the inn was well looked after. It would certainly be more amenable than a farmhouse, and she was with her grandfather. After a few more seconds hesitation, she nodded her head. 'But if we stop here, there will be no time to go further. And we can stay for half an hour only.'

She ignored Dougal's muttered, 'Hae she aywis bin this high an' mighty?' and climbed down from the carriage.

'Will Percy and Finn wonder where we've gone?' she asked, picking her way across the yard. Fortunately, with all the dry weather, there was no mud to contend with.

'The barouche is still there, and Finn's got more than fresh air between his ears, even if old Percy hasn't.' Rosie winced internally at his words. Good manners were not high on her grandfather's list of priorities.

Seconds later, she followed the two men into the dimness of the inn. Despite being in a relatively quiet location, the bar was both clean and well appointed. Clearly, the inn's business came from the higher echelons of society. However, being mid-afternoon, they were its only patrons.

Roseanna and Dougal seated themselves at a table near to a huge fireplace. A fire was well established, despite it being August, and in truth Rosie was glad of it. With its small windows and dark interior, the room didn't hold much warmth. Flossy and Trixie too wasted no time before stretching out in front of it.

After a few minutes, the innkeeper bustled in. After briefly eying the clergyman's cassock in surprise, he murmured, 'What can I get for you, Reverend?' just as Percy walked in. Roseanna found herself stifling a chuckle at the man's subsequent alarmed expression.

'Have you seen Finn?' the curate asked, hurrying to the table.

'Nae, he hasnae come in here.' Dougal gave a nonchalant shrug. 'Ah dinnae think ye hae any cause tae worry. The lad's likely off explorin'.'

Percy frowned, looking around. He knew Finn was well able to look after himself, but it was hard not to worry, nonetheless.

The Reverend brought back two small brandies, a whisky for Dougal and a glass of lemonade each for Rosie and Finn.

Dougal eyed the pale liquid in his glass with distaste and shook his head. 'Ah dinnae ken where he foond this rubbish. Mebbe he made it hisself.'

'Stop whining,' the Reverend growled. 'Next time you can buy your own deuced whisky.'

'An ye tell me, what daes a Sassenach God botherer ken aboot it? Yer wouldnae ken a good whisky an it hit ye on ur thick heid.'

Rosie looked on worriedly as her grandfather drew himself up, clearly preparing to give the Scot a blistering set down. Fortunately, however, before the argument had the chance to escalate, Finn came running in.

'There be a furren nob upstairs,' he announced, sitting down and picking up his lemonade.

'How do you know he's foreign?' the Reverend asked, ignoring the boy's repetition of his earlier derogatory comment.

Finn thought for a second, slurping his drink noisily. 'Ah reckon he might hae bin one o' them frogs,' he said at length. 'He wa' dressed all in black like somebodie be deid an' he sounded funny.'

'Was he alone?' the Reverend asked. Fin nodded.

'That fella o'er there took him up some cheese, an' ah heard the frog ask aboot two men he wa' waitin' fer.' The boy cast a hopeful look towards the bar. 'Ah wouldnae say nae tae some cheese. Ah be fair starvin'.'

'Do you think it could be the Comte?' Rosie asked her grandfather, her voice half anxious, half excited.

'Well, sounding funny isn't any surety that the fellow's French,' the Reverend replied, 'but mayhap we need to investigate.'

'I'm not sure that's wise, Sir,' Percy protested. 'I don't know who this Frenchman is, but evidently you and Lady Roseanna do. And from the tone of your voice, he's no gentleman.'

'Ah could fancy a pickled trotter...'

'Who be this man, Augustus?' Dougal stared pointedly at the Reverend, eyes narrowed.

'Or mebbe a few pickled herrings...'

'Is there something you haven't shared with me, Sir?' Percy sounded as though his heart was about to break.

'Thunder an' turf, Percy, I don't tell you *everything*.' The Reverend's voice was defensive – a sure sign he was either lying or felt guilty. In the curate's experience, it was most likely both.

'Or a nice bit o' pie...'

Watching the interaction between the three men, Roseanna had no idea what to do, and she could see the same indecision in her grandfather's eyes.

Telling Percy and Dougal about the possible conspiracy would be breaking their word to the Duke – not to mention potentially causing the very issue her uncle had been trying to avoid.

But on the other hand, if it *was* the Comte d'Ansouis upstairs, he might well be meeting the same two men she'd overheard in the Duke's study. If she was able to put face to each of the voices… Her thoughts screeched to a halt. How the devil could they even hope to get close enough to discover d'Ansouis' intentions? And if the Comte was as dangerous as Tristan seemed to think, any attempt would be entirely too risky. Especially as they had an eight-year-old boy and two small dogs with them.

'Ah ken they hae some pickled walnuts…'

'Unfortunately, if I tell you more, I will be breaking a confidence,' her grandfather was saying between gritted teeth.

'In that case, involving ourselves in any kind of espionage activity would be foolhardy in the extreme.' Percy's voice was unusually firm.

Without warning, Dougal consumed the rest of his whisky. 'Dinnae fash yersel, gentlemen,' he announced, slamming his glass back onto the table, 'Dougal Galbraith be here. An ah be jest the man ye need fer a spot o' snoopin'.'

'If ye find me curled up intae a ball an' dried up like one o' them mummy things, it'll be because ah've *starved tae death*…'

# Sixteen

Etienne Babin gritted his teeth. He was so damn close to the fruition of his plan. He'd never imagined just how long it would take to reduce the country he secretly loathed to the kind of anarchy he envisioned. But, finally, *finally*, the end was in sight.

He bit into the cheese with a grimace, then spat it out onto his plate. He'd lived for over twenty years in a country full of dull peasants with no more appreciation of good food than a monkey. Where the most important thing was to boil the vegetables until they were a soft pulp, just in case a guest arrived without his teeth.

Babin sneered, taking a sip of his red wine. This, at least, had come from France.

Leaning back in his chair, he swirled the ruby liquid in his glass. If he was being completely honest with himself, the Etienne Babin who'd escaped France all those years ago would have had no more appreciation of good wine than the average English bourgeoisie.

. . .

He'd acquired his love of good things from the real Comte d'Ansouis. Babin sighed and raised his glass to his mentor - fifteen years in an unmarked grave. Pierre had taught him everything he knew. He'd turned him from a thug to a learned man. From a sans-culotte to a cultured émigré with impeccable taste. He owed d'Ansouis everything. Even his name.

But unfortunately, the real Comte did not nurse hatred. The fool wanted to be remembered as a *philanthrope*.

Babin did not simply *nurse* hatred, he *thrived* on it. In the end, he'd broken the nobleman's neck and taken his identity. It had been surprisingly easy. Their build was not dissimilar - good food and comfortable living had restored some of the Comte's natural bulk. But more importantly, they'd lived in isolation. D'Ansouis had an almost irrational fear of being dragged back to France – a fear he never really lost. At first, Babin had told himself he was doing d'Ansouis a service in putting him out of his misery. But eventually he stopped caring.

He had a purpose. He had a plan. He wanted to make the world suffer as he had. And that meant *all* the self-important bastards. The *Revisionists* saw him as their saviour, heralding in a brighter dawn.

Babin chuckled. He had no interest in creating a new, better world order. He just wanted to destroy the old one. Fortunately, his co-conspirators didn't know that - yet.

This worthless country was of no consequence, and the sooner its inhabitants realised that fact, the better.

. . .

Indeed, by Monday, life for the people of Great Britain would never be the same again.

~

'Can ye remember what the windows in the room looked oot ontae?'

'Ah didnae gae intae the room. Ah only peeked through the door.' Finn thought for a second before adding, 'Ah reckon there be a tree ootside one o' 'em. Somethin' wi' bright berries.'

They were standing at the rear of the inn. Unlike most establishments relying on wealthy, overnight travellers, there was a garden of sorts. To one side stood the privy Percy had used earlier, but even though they were relatively close, the smell didn't quite require a kerchief to the nose.

Percy was standing protectively over Finn, determined that this time that the lad wouldn't be dragged into any smoky business. Despite that, the curate found himself discussing the odds for the position of the Comte's private room.

'It's got to be that one,' the Reverend declared. 'If Finn was at the door, so...' he moved into the imagined position, 'then the only room he could possibly see the tree from would be that one.' He pointed to the window directly above them.

'We can't stand here all day,' Roseanna interrupted in a heated whisper, when it looked as though Dougal was about to argue.

'Aye, ye be right, lass. We need tae strike while the iron be hot.'

. . .

'We'll never get up there. There's nothing to hold on to and my days of climbing walls and scaling ramparts are over,' the Reverend declared sadly.

'As I remember, Sir, I was the one who did most of the climbing and scaling.' Percy's words were quite resolute, and Roseanna found herself looking at the curate in a new light. Whenever she'd previously been in his company, he'd seemed such a modest, reserved man.

"I can't argue with that, Percy,' Reverend Shackleford answered with a sigh. 'Though, being a natural chucklehead, you've always needed a fair bit of encouragement. And I can't deny that all those times you got banged on the noggin have turned you a bit strange on occasion.'

'Ah reckon we could use a ladder,' Finn hissed from behind the privy. None of them had noticed the lad had wandered off.

'And where do you think we'll find a deuced ladder?' the Reverend retorted.

'Right here!' Finn bent down and lifted up the end of a rickety ladder that looked as though it had last been used in the Norman Conquest.

'That be jest what we need,' Dougal crowed, hurrying over to help the boy. Together, they dragged the ladder back to where the others were clustered. 'Dinnae jest stand there, gie us a hand.'

. . .

After about five minutes and a few muttered curses, they managed to get the ladder propped against the wall. It was about a foot short of the window. 'Perfect.' Dougal rubbed his hands together. 'Right then, Augustus, you and Percy hold the bottom o' the ladder steady an' ah'll climb up there an' hae a listen tae what the bampot haes tae say.'

'You can't be the one going up there,' Reverend Shackleford hissed. 'You won't understand anything you hear.'

The Scot gave him a baffled frown. 'What daes that matter? Ah'm nae daft.'

'Well, that's a matter up for debate,' the Reverend muttered under his breath as Dougal stepped on the first rung, which promptly snapped under his weight.

'Ah'm nae hurt, dinnae fash yersels.'

'You're only on the first deuced rung,' Reverend Shackleford scoffed.

Fortunately, the next rung held, as did the one above that. Inch by careful inch, Dougal made his way up the ladder. Finally, with only two rungs above him, the old Scot carefully reached out for the windowsill.

'Be careful,' Rosie called softly, hardly daring to look.

Gripping the sill, Dougal pulled himself up until he was standing on the next but last rung and could finally see through the window.

'There be three men in there,' he hissed, pressing his nose against the glass.

'Be careful they don't see you,' Percy warned from the bottom of the ladder.

'They be arguing aboot somethin'.'

'What are they saying?' The Reverend called up.

'Ah cannae hear o'er yer blatherin''

The Reverend gritted his teeth but remained silent.

Dougal suddenly bent his head, causing the ladder to wobble dangerously. 'One o' the men be leavin the room,' he hissed urgently.

Roseanna's heart lurched. If either of the men were traitors in her uncle's household, it was imperative they could be recognised again. She doubted very much that Dougal would be able to see much looking through murky glass into a darkened room, but if the man was going outside, she might get the chance to see his face.

She looked over at her grandfather and Percy. Both men were entirely focused on the Scot. Without giving herself any more time to question her common sense, Rosie tapped Finn on the shoulder, putting her finger to her lips as he turned to look at her. Without speaking, she handed him the two lead handles, then pointed to herself and the direction she intended to go. When he stepped forward to go with her, she shook her head and pointed to the two clergymen. The boy pouted, but followed it with a small nod.

Seconds later, she was hurrying round the side of the inn. She did not know where the man was going. In truth, he might have nothing to do with the Comte d'Ansouis or the *Revisionists*. But in her opinion, they couldn't afford to take that chance.

As she approached a large archway out to the inn's front yard, Rosie slowed down, giving herself time to tidy her hair and smooth down her skirts. A lone dishevelled woman would be more likely to attract attention. Then, taking a deep breath, she stepped through the archway.

Unfortunately, unlike earlier, the inn's front yard was now quite busy with ostlers. She could see Thomas dozing up on his box, and the unknown carriage was still there. The horses were now eating grain from nosebags, but the fact that they'd still not been unharnessed was a good indication of their owner's imminent return. Certainly, whoever it was had no intention of staying overnight.

Rosie felt her stomach clench. Her gut told her she hadn't got long. Glancing round, she looked for the presence of another conveyance and, after a few seconds, spotted a small dog cart with a lone horse. That had to be it. She stepped behind their barouche, careful not to wake Thomas. From there, she had a good view of anyone returning to the cart.

As she waited, she began to wonder if she'd got it entirely wrong. The man had had more than enough time to get from the upstairs room to the yard. It could be that he'd just gone to fetch food and drink. And it wasn't only that. She couldn't imagine how the two men had managed to leave Blackmore if they were posing as servants.

Cursing herself for making foolish assumptions, Rosie took a step towards the cart, thinking she may as well have a quick look seeing as it didn't look as though her quarry was coming. After checking she wasn't being observed, she continued on, making sure to tread confidently, as if she had every right to be there. As she approached, the horse tossed his head, but didn't resist when she stroked his nose. Was he one of the Duke's? He was clearly well looked after, but she couldn't remember seeing him in Blackmore's stable.

Worrying anxiously at her bottom lip, Roseanna stepped round the horse and studied the cart. There was nothing on the side to give an indication of who it belonged to, but that didn't really mean anything. A sudden thought struck her. Had either man spotted their barouche? And if they had, would they have recognised the crest? Rosie sucked in her breath, fighting a surge of panic. They either hadn't seen it, or they were nothing to do with Blackmore.

Sensing she was running out of time, Roseanna looked down into the cart. There was nothing but an old piece of cloth. Leaning down, she lifted one corner, feeling a surge of disappointment when she realised there was nothing underneath it. She was just about to turn away when she caught sight of what looked like the corner of a piece of paper sticking up between the wooden slats. Heart pounding, she raised herself up onto her tiptoes and leaned almost fully into the cart. Just as she feared she was about to overbalance, she managed to catch hold of it between her forefinger and thumb. Fortunately, as she pushed herself backwards, the rest of the sheet came up through the slats with only the smallest of tears.

. . .

Without looking to see what was on it, she hurriedly folded it into quarters and tucked it into her reticule. Then, keeping her head down, she started walking quickly back towards the archway.

'What do you think you're doing?' The shout from behind her was unexpected and shocking. Clearly, she'd been so absorbed in retrieving the sheet of paper, she'd neglected to check her surroundings.

For a second, Roseanna's whole body froze, her mind a complete blank. Then, swallowing in fear, she slowly turned. Even in her terror, her eyes automatically took in the greying hair, pebble eyes and sagging gut.

'I said what do you think you...' His voice was suddenly interrupted by a loud yell from behind her.

'There ye be Fiona. Mam's bin lookin fer yer everywhere. Hoo many times hae she told ye tae nae wander off.' Finn appeared at her side and grabbed her arm.

'Ah be sorry, Maister. Ma sister be awa in the heid, an it be ma job tae look after her.' He glanced up at his *sister*, and finally recovering her wits, Rosie obligingly stuck out her tongue and tried to tug her arm away.

'Ye gaunnie nae dae that,' Finn scolded her, steadily dragging her backwards. 'We be gaun back tae Mam an' that be that.' He raised an apologetic hand towards the man, who was now staring at them in bemusement. 'She'll nae be botherin' ye agin, Maister.' Then, still gripping Rosie's arm, he steered her determinedly back towards the archway.

. . .

As soon as they were out of sight, Rosie turned to the grinning boy and, without warning, gave him a hug.

'Och, ye gaunnie nae dae that,' Finn repeated, squirming away, his face red with embarrassment.

'You were wonderful,' Rosie smiled. 'I'd have been in dreadful trouble if you hadn't intervened. Where are Trixie and Flossy?' She became aware of a distant barking. 'Please tell me you didn't lock them in the privy?'

Finn gave her a disbelieving look. 'Ye think ah be daft? O' course ah didnae. They be wi' the Revren.'

Feeling an abrupt sense of foreboding, Rosie gave him another small smile before picking up her skirts and hastening back to the others.

She was just about to turn the corner into the small garden when the two dogs hurtled into view. She heard a muffled, 'Oot the way ye eejit Sassenach God walloper,' followed by the sudden appearance of the top of the ladder. That in itself would have been little cause for worry, except that Dougal was still clinging to the top of it.

## Seventeen

If there was one thing Augustus Shackleford didn't do well, it was waiting. And, as it happened, standing at the bottom of a ladder. What made it worse on this occasion was looking at Percy's serene expression not two feet away. Well, that and the fact that he was currently battling an irrational urge to plant a prime facer right on the end of his curate's even-tempered nose.

Gritting his teeth, the Reverend looked back up the ladder where Dougal still had his ear pressed against the grimy windowpane. Of course, this could all be a deuced waste of time. 'Anything?' he called up.

Dougal looked down. 'Ah cannae hear much, but ah ken he be a ne'er-dae-weel. That much be certain. An' one o' his flunkie's called him *yer ludship*. Ah'd hear more if ah could open the bloody window.'

'Has the other fellow come back yet?' Dougal shook his head, causing the ladder to wobble ominously. Startled, Percy clutched at his half, his serene expression vanishing faster than the congregation when the collection box went round.

The Reverend was about to give a very unchristianly snigger, when he suddenly noticed his granddaughter was missing. 'Where's Rosie?' he demanded, feeling suddenly lightheaded.

'Ah reckon she gaed tae look fer the fella,' Finn answered.

'Thunder an' turf,' Augustus Shackleford moaned. 'You need to come down now,' he hissed up to Dougal. 'Roseanna's done a runner.'

'Ah'll gae and look fer her,' Finn offered, stepping forward. 'Dinnae fash yerself, Revren. Ye stay here an' look after the dogs.' He handed the distraught clergyman the two leads, then before anyone had the chance to argue, sprinted off round the corner.

Naturally, by this point, any calmness Percy had been feeling promptly disappeared, and the curate let go of the ladder, about to run after his adopted son - unfortunately, at exactly the same moment that Dougal was easing his hands from the windowsill and lowering one foot down to the next rung of the ladder. The Scot uttered a panicked yell as the ladder wobbled, leaving his foot swinging in midair.

With a gasp, Percy grabbed hold of his side again and slowly the ladder steadied. 'Get a deuced move on,' the Reverend shouted up, completely abandoning any efforts at keeping the noise down. Carefully, Dougal stepped down onto the next rung and managed to get a grip on the top of the ladder.

But before he could go any further, the window above him was suddenly thrust open. Thinking they'd been discovered, all three men pressed themselves against the wall. After a few moments when no shout was forthcoming, the Reverend lifted his head and gave Dougal the thumbs up, just as a voice from inside the room thundered, '*Merde*, you are both *imbéciles*. You had one job. *One*.'

Sadly, neither Flossy nor Trixie knew the difference between harmless and non-harmless yelling, and at the sound of the strident voice, both dogs set up a cacophony of barking and dashed under the bottom rung of the ladder. It might have gone reasonably well had the Reverend been able to extract himself from the handles before the dogs had got further than a lead's length on the other side, but unfortunately said handles were firmly looped around his wrist.

With a surprised 'woomph,' the Reverend found himself squashed up against the ladder, which slowly began to slide. Frantically, Percy fumbled to free the loops stuck around the Reverend's wrist, finally managing to slide them off, just as Dougal shouted a hoarse, 'Oot the way ye eejit Sassenach God walloper.'

Falling backwards, the two clergymen watched helplessly as the ladder slowly toppled with the Scot desperately hanging onto its top.

Roseanna gasped, coming to a halt as she watched the ladder fell inexorably towards a large oak tree. Seconds later, it crashed into the branches, just as her grandfather and Percy appeared round the corner.

Dougal had completely disappeared from view, and all three humans rushed over to the tree, staring anxiously up into its branches. For a few horrible seconds, there was nothing at all, then all of a sudden there was a rustle and a muttered, 'Ah think ah might hae broken ma big toe.'

※

'Well, I think we can confidentially say that he was the blackguard we were looking for,' Reverend Shackleford commented as they finally left the inn behind. 'But we're still none the wiser about what the varmint is up to.'

'Dae ye think noo ah nearly lost ma foot, ye can tell us wha' bloody flumgummery yer involved in?'

'You didn't nearly lose your deuced foot,' Reverend Shackleford retorted. 'You've lost the nail on your big toe.'

'Aye, but it couldhae bin the end o' me. Ye could hae bin puttin' me in a box right noo.'

'I agree with Dougal, Sir,' Percy interrupted. 'We cannot be expected to risk our lives for a cause we have no knowledge of.'

The Reverend sighed. The days were long gone when his curate hung on his every word and blindly followed his every edict. In fact, these days, Percy was more the reverend than he was.

'I do think we should tell them, Grandpapa.' Roseanna's voice was quiet, but resolved, clearly stating her position on the matter. If he didn't enlighten them, then she would.

It actually took until they turned onto the Blackmore road for the Reverend to tell the complete story – mainly because everyone kept interrupting. 'I truly have no idea what will happen now,' the clergyman finished. 'Rosie and I will report back to the Duke. I will, of course, tell him that I've broken his confidence, but I th...'

'... *You* didn't Grandpapa, *we* did,' Roseanna interrupted firmly.

The clergyman nodded, his eyes unexpectedly filling with tears. 'In the circumstances, I believe we have done the right thing.'

'Be there any treasure?' Finn blurted as the barouche stopped outside the vicarage.

～

By the time Rosie climbed out of the carriage, she felt as if she'd been hung out to dry. She asked Thomas to continue on to the stables, thinking to give Trixie time to do her business before looking for her uncle. She felt as though she'd been away for hours and hours, though in truth, it was less than four. When they left, the Comte was still at the inn. She didn't know how much he'd seen or heard, but she knew one of his henchmen would likely recognise her if he saw her again. Still, there was nothing she could do about that now.

Picking up the little dog, she went first to the kitchen to ask Mrs Higgins if she had any leftovers for Trixie's dinner. To her surprise, the kitchen was chaotic. Standing at the entrance, Rosie frowned, watching the staff running around. There was an underlying sense of panic. Clearly, something had happened since she left after lunch.

After a few minutes, Mrs Higgins caught sight of her. 'Why are you here, milady? Shouldn't you be at the meeting?'

Roseanna felt an uncomfortable sense of isolation. 'I've been out for the afternoon, Mrs Higgins, so I'm afraid I'm a little behind. What meeting is that?'

'Why, the one to discuss the news, milady. The whole family will be there.'

'And what news would that be?'

The head cook looked at her as though she was addled, then shook her head and went to get Trixie some scraps for her dinner. Seconds later, the matron handed them over and touched Rosie's arm. 'Get yourself to the large drawing room as soon as you can, milady. The King is coming to Blackmore tomorrow.'

∽

Roseanna felt unaccountably nervous as she knocked on the door to the large drawing room. Initially, she thought it hadn't been heard, but after about half a minute, the door was pulled open. 'Roseanna Atwood, you be surely a sight fer sore eyes.' Malcolm stepped forward and pulled her into the room.

Blinking, Rosie looked round. After a few seconds, she realised the whole family was in the room. Every adult member. The only two missing were her grandparents. And of course, Dougal Galbraith.

Completely unaccustomed to being the centre of attention, Roseanna stepped back, clutching Trixie to her, just as another knock sounded. Seconds later, she stared incredulously as the old Scot was ushered into the room.

'I think that's everyone,' Nicholas declared as the door shut. 'I will fill Augustus and Agnes in later.'

'Thank you for coming. I know it wasn't too onerous since you were all in the house anyway, but still...' He paused, giving a dark chuckle. Grace took his hand as he continued. 'Some of you might be aware that I've been a little distracted since you all arrived for this year's garden party. You can rest assured that I've had good reason.' He paused again as Malcolm handed him a brandy, then gave a rueful laugh. 'I hope you've all got a drink of some description, because believe me ladies and gentlemen, you're going to need it...'

It took the Duke around twenty minutes to describe the events of the last week. Roseanna noted that he went into very little detail about the *Revisionists*, only that the group existed, and the Comte was suspected to be their leader. When he spoke about Tristan Bernart's real reason for being at Blackmore, Rosie felt a ridiculous sense of pride as she watched him step forward and incline his head.

'And now, to add another level of farce to this already preposterous tale, if you're not already aware, King William will be arriving on the morrow. So, not only will we have the suspected leader of a group of conspiracists and two warring politicians on opposite sides of the Reform Bill in residence this weekend, but Royalty as well.'

The resulting silence was deafening. There couldn't have been a person in the room who wasn't aware of the disaster they were teetering on.

It was Dougal Galbraith who spoke first. 'Well, laddie, ah hae tae admit, ah can totally understand why ye wanted me oot o' the way.'

⁓

Roseanna went to put Trixie in her bedchamber after the meeting, even though she knew her parents and sister would be waiting to speak with her. In truth, she felt so far out of her depth; she was in grave danger of drowning. Her life up to now had been sheltered – she was only now realising just how much. Intrigue had played no part unless it had been on the stage and now, here she was, neck deep in it. Sighing, she put Trixie down on the floor and fed her the scraps Mrs Higgins had given her. Her uncle had asked to see her as soon as was convenient. She gave a dark chuckle. Doubtless, he wasn't expecting her to report anything much at all. She rummaged around in her reticule for the sheet of paper she'd found in the dogcart. There had been no time to even look at it, and in all honesty, she'd almost forgotten she had it. Seating herself on the bed, she unfolded the sheet and found herself looking at a detailed plan of Blackmore.

'Did I tell them enough?'

'Aye, yer grace. I dinnae think pouring oil ontae an already volatile situation is likely to help any.' Malcolm sighed as he sat down on the other side of the desk. 'In fairness, they reacted well to what ye did tell them.'

'Well, it's not as if the family is entirely unused to dealing with unbelievable situations,' Nicholas responded drily.

Malcolm chuckled. 'I cannae argue with ye there, Nick.'

The two men were alone in the Duke's study, which was rapidly becoming the *hub of operations*. There had still been no word of the Comte's arrival and the sense of doom that had plagued Nicholas ever since he'd agreed to dupe d'Ansouis was beginning to reach epic proportions. In truth, he'd been a fool to get involved, but the original plan had been simple enough. He just hadn't foreseen how events would spiral out of control, though clearly, he should have done.

Still, regrets were useless. The past could not be changed, and he had to play the hand he'd been dealt. But never had his responsibilities weighed so heavily.

'Dinnae berate yerself, laddie,' Malcolm murmured. His comment elicited a wan smile. The Scot knew him almost better than anyone.

'I shou...' the Duke's response was cut short by a knock on the door. 'Come,' he shouted instead.

Roseanna stepped nervously into the room, wondering if she'd ever become comfortable in her stern uncle's presence.

Nevertheless, moments later, she forgot her anxiety as she related the events of the afternoon. Indeed, watching the Duke's and Malcolm's faces become more and more incredulous, she actually fought the urge to giggle. It had all been so surreal and felt even more so now. In fairness, she was careful to make light of the fear she'd felt at being spotted in the inn's yard.

'In truth, if they are servants here, I cannot fathom how they managed to absent themselves for so long. However, I'm certain I would recognise the man by the cart if I saw him again...' She paused before adding, 'Naturally, I'm concerned that he will also recognise me.'

'I doubt he'd recognise ye if he saw ye here, lass,' Malcolm reassured her. 'In my experience, people see what they expect tae see. Finn's interference made ye into a young Scottish lass who's a little simple – and that's how he'll remember ye. So, what did this varmint look like?'

'He had grey hair, tied back with some string. His face was pasty, a little like uncooked dough, and his eyes were small and set deep. He had a paunch, and his shirt was clearly too tight.' She paused, thinking for a second. 'It didn't look particularly clean either, and neither did his breeches.' She turned to the Duke. 'Now I come to think about it, there was a peculiar smell about him. It was in the cart too, though I only smelt it very faintly when I nearly fell in.'

'He sounds very prepossessing,' the Duke murmured drily. 'If he looked so slovenly, it's unlikely he's employed in the house. I think perhaps we should concentrate our search on the outside staff. I'll circulate his particulars to the others.'

'Do you want me to look for him?' Roseanna asked.

The Duke shook his head. 'Keep an eye out for him, certainly, and if you do happen to spot him, then please tell me or Malcolm immediately. But whatever you do, please don't go searching for him.'

Malcolm nodded in agreement. 'Ye mustnae put yerself in harm's way lass – any more than you have already at least. Yer father will string us up himself should any hurt come tae ye. Now, what did ye find in the cart?'

In answer, Rosie opened the piece of paper and laid it on the desk.

The Duke frowned, picking it up. 'It's a plan of Blackmore,' he stated flatly after a few seconds.

'I think it's important to them,' Rosie responded. 'Grandpapa, Percy and Dougal all heard the Comte shouting at the two men about something, and I think the reason may well have been the loss of this.' She looked between the two men. 'Could they have been looking for it when I overheard them?'

Nicholas looked down at the plan. 'Well, if they were, this isn't it. This one is crude at best and there are several errors.' He handed the sheet to Malcolm and climbed to his feet, going over to a large cupboard. 'This is always kept locked when I'm not in the room,' he said, pulling open both doors. 'And the lock is new. Only the very best rum dubber would stand any chance of picking it.' He pulled out a rolled-up sheaf of papers, adding, 'and possibly Patience.'

Returning to the table with the bundle under his arm, Nicholas caught sight of his niece's baffled look. He gave a soft laugh as he spread the sheets out on the desk. 'Your Aunt Patience has quite a few less than ladylike skills, Rosie. When all this is over, I heartily recommend you ask her about them.'

'She'll nae thank ye fer bringing that up,' Malcolm warned.

'I know,' Nicholas responded, losing his grim expression for a few seconds. To Rosie, it made him seem infinitely more approachable. She looked over at the sheet on the top of the pile he'd laid out. 'These are the original detailed plans. They could well be what the thieves were looking for. The question is, why?'

'Well, if they're looking tae murder occupants in their beds, they'd need more than just a plan o' the house.'

'They'd need to know which room their victim or victims are in.'

'But surely one without the other is useless to them?' Roseanna countered.

'They'd need both,' Malcolm clarified.

'We have to assume d'Ansouis is already in possession of the list of guests and their proposed rooms,' Nicholas bit out, 'so he knows Wellington and Grey will be here.'

'He'll be cock-a-hoop when he finds out the King is coming,' Malcolm growled.

'God's teeth,' Nicholas swore, 'Somehow, we're going to have to root out these damned traitors before the King gets here. D'Ansouis will hang for this, if I have to do it myself.'

'I think ye need to send a message tae Chapman,' Malcolm declared. 'He and his men more than proved themselves when we were at Caerlaverock. If we cannae apprehend these bastards – my apologies Rosie – before Wellington and Grey's arrival, at the very least they'll need extra protection. I'm assuming the King will have his own guards.'

'Chapman already has his men on standby,' Nicholas returned, 'and I don't think we can assume anything at this stage. Making assumptions is part of the reason we're in this deuced mess.'

'We no longer have the luxury of playing the long game,' he continued. 'Tristan will need to show his hand as soon as he can do so without arousing suspicion. Whether we like it or not, things will come to a head at Blackmore.'

'They're going to need another plan of the house, though,' Malcolm warned, so we need to search *every room*. Likely someone here made this one, and while it may not be completely accurate, it's close enough.

Both men were now ignoring Rosie, and she was entirely content for them to do so. Indeed, she found their conversation terrifying and wanted nothing more than to take to her bed and stay there until it was all over. She was just wondering how to excuse herself when a knock sounded on the door. Seconds later, Boscastle informed his grace that the Comte d'Ansouis had arrived.

# Eighteen

Readying herself for dinner, Roseanna was only half listening to her twin prattling on. Francesca seemed little perturbed about the possible ramifications of having a potential traitor staying in the same house. She was far more focused on the fact that the King was coming to stay. The danger seemed to have largely gone over her head.

But then, she would very likely have been the same if it hadn't been for her unexpected encounter with Tristan Bernard and the subsequent temptation to eavesdrop.

She wondered what he was doing now. Was he still with the Comte since he was to act as the nobleman's valet? She knew Tristan's role was to try to draw the man out as quickly as possible, and that made his position especially dangerous. He might as well have drawn a bullet hole in the middle of his forehead and written *shoot here* underneath it.

Feeling a clutch of fear, Rosie turned towards her sister, determined to put such worries aside - at least until dinner. She couldn't imagine that any of them would be seated anywhere near the Comte. That burden would undoubtedly be left to the older members of the family. She didn't know whether to be impressed or concerned that her aunts and uncles were so accomplished at weaving Canterbury tales.

'Do you think these pearls look a little insipid against the orange taffeta?' Francesca was asking her. 'I had thought to wear the emerald gown, but once I realised the King would be here tomorrow.' The two women had elected to help each other get ready since Doris and Emily, their two lady's maids from Northwood, were now being shared with Aunt Faith and Henrietta.

'You look gorgeous,' Roseanna responded. And she meant it. Francesca might not be conventionally beautiful, but her vivaciousness drew people to her.

In response, Francesca threw her arms around her twin. 'I've missed you these last days and I'm so pleased you no longer have to spend all of your time with Grandpapa minding Mr Galbraith.'

Roseanna opened her mouth to disagree, then closed it again. Presumably, since the stakes were now so high, the Duke and Duchess believed they could rely on Dougal to keep out of trouble without supervision. Having spent the last few hours with the old Scot, Rosie admired their optimism. If the opportunity arose, she'd have a quiet word with her grandfather after dinner. She absently clipped on her earrings.

'Oh, they look perfect, dearest.' At her sister's words, Roseanna creased her brow in confusion. Then she realised she'd been wool-gathering again. Zounds, she really needed to gather herself together. She looked down at her pale lemon gown. In all honesty, she'd chosen it because she always felt it helped her fade into the background. It certainly wasn't one of her favourites. But the daffodil earrings she'd paired with it always felt so cheerful.

She smiled and picked up her reticule. 'Would you take this down for me? I have to take Trixie out and I know I'll simply forget it when I come back up.'

Francesca nodded. 'Are you sure you don't want me to come with you?' she asked. 'I don't think Uncle Nicholas wishes us to walk around the house alone... just in case. And I know how prone you are to wandering off.'

'I'll be perfectly well, sweet. Please don't worry. I have no intention of lingering. As soon as Trixie's seen to her ablutions, I'll bring her back here and join you.' She clipped the little dog's lead on while she was speaking

'Well, don't take too long,' Frankie warned. 'You know very well that Mama wishes to speak with you and since you've got back this afternoon, you've been fudging.'

Roseanna winced, then sighed. 'I'll speak with her as soon as I come down,' she promised, linking her arm in her twin's. Francesca gave her an arch look. 'I don't think you'll have much choice dearest. Mama is determined to corner you, and the last thing we want is for her to raise her voice...'

For once, Rosie did not linger in the kitchen garden. Although the hour was still relatively early, the shadows already hid large swathes, intensifying her unease. Despite Malcolm's reassurance, the thought that she might be recognised was terrifying. Trixie too picked up on her disquiet and didn't waste time sniffing before squatting down to water the dandelions.

Picking up the little dog, she glanced up at the faceless house. She could see candlelight through many of the windows, and in any other circumstance, she would have found it welcoming, but now she couldn't help wondering about the unseen hands holding the flickering candles. Was somebody standing out of sight, watching her?

Gritting her teeth, Roseanna hurried back towards the open door, only for a figure to step out of the shadows just before she reached it. Stumbling back, she only just managed to stifle a cry as the urgent voice of Tristan Bernart whispered, 'My lady, don't scream.'

Trixie grumbled in her arms but didn't begin barking, and Rosie calmed her with shaking fingers before placing her back down on the ground.

'His grace told me what happened today,' Tristan whispered. 'I wished to make sure you weren't harmed.'

'You scared me half to death,' Roseanna accused, ignoring his question. 'What are you doing out here? I thought you were with the Comte.'

'I've just left him,' Tristan answered. 'I was hoping you'd bring your dog out here.'

'I wasn't hurt,' she admitted. 'More scared than anything. My foolish impulse could have ended in disaster.'

'But you found the plans they had of Blackmore,' the footman argued. 'We suspected d'Ansouis intended something for this weekend, but now we know for sure. We just need to catch the bastard in the act.' He didn't apologise for the expletive.

'What is the Comte like?' Rosie asked curiously. 'Do you think him dicked in the nob?'

Tristan eyed her for a second, wondering at the question. Then he remembered she knew nothing of his former life and had no idea he and Babin had shared a cell together.

'He's a charlatan,' Tris answered shortly. 'And an arrogant one at that.'

'Do you think he is planning something for this weekend?'

'Most assuredly. But it's not just d'Ansouis we have to stop. We need to smash the whole conspiracy wide open before they get the chance to do something heinous.'

He stepped forward, close enough that she could feel the heat of him. She gazed up into his face, inscrutable in the twilight, and suddenly felt a longing so acute, it nearly brought her to her knees.

'I... I... do not think you should stand so close,' she murmured, staring directly at his chest, inches from her face.

'I have a house,' he declared abruptly, his voice almost gruff. She lifted her head, finally allowing her eyes to meet his. Why was he telling her this?

'It's in Torquay, close to Redstone House. Roan Carew and I are neighbours.'

'That's nice,' she managed after a few seconds, trying to make sense of his words. 'I like Torquay.' For some reason, her answer elicited a rueful smile. Then he briefly closed his eyes.

'I have to get back,' he murmured when he opened them again. She nodded, then for some strange reason, felt a desperate need to touch his warmth. Without thinking, she lifted her hand and pressed it against his chest. The reaction was instant.

His hands came up to grip her shoulders and, with a soft expletive, his lips came down on hers. For a second, she remained still. The feel of his full lips pressed against hers was like *nothing* she'd ever felt before. Indeed, she'd never imagined a man's lips could feel so soft. He did not move. Did nothing but waited, holding her pressed against him. She knew he would not force her, though she could feel his body, taut and hard underneath the stillness. She sensed his restraint, his *need*. And she could not have stepped away if the devil himself had appeared.

Instinct told her what to do next. Hesitantly, she opened her mouth and with a groan, he deepened the kiss, his tongue slipping in to tangle with hers, his mouth plundering, demanding. She should have been afraid, but when his hands slipped from her shoulders to splay across her back, she willingly allowed him to press her against that most intimate part of him, sliding her own hands up around his neck as she stood up on her toes, better able to ride the hardness she could feel pressing between her legs.

Her whole body felt on fire. Her breasts were crushed against his chest, but as she moved, her nipples tingled as they rubbed against the roughness of his jacket.

Then suddenly, shockingly, it was over. It took him seconds to slide his hands from her back, grip either side of her waist, and set her from him. They were both panting hard. Unconsciously, Roseanna took a step forward. 'Don't,' he groaned harshly, and she stopped uncertainly, wondering if she'd done something wrong.

'If you come any closer, I will be tempted to lift your skirts and take you where you stand,' Tristan murmured crudely. But instead of horrifying her, his words sent a stab of longing directly into her core. Roseanna didn't move, but stared wordlessly into his silver eyes, heavy lidded with desire.

'Your family will be waiting for you,' he growled, and she gasped as reality finally came rushing back. How long had she been out here? Frankie would be worried sick about her. And damn it, where was Trixie? A stab of fear dissolved the last of her ardour and she swung round, desperately looking for the little dog, only to spot her seconds later sitting next to the door, nonchalantly scratching behind her ear.

Almost crying with relief, Roseanna rushed to pick the animal up. Now that reality had intruded, she hardly dared to look at Tristan. Truly, he must think her a harlot.

She was aware that he was saying something, but in her agitation, she had no idea what. All she wanted to do now was escape. Clutching the little dog to her, she pulled open the door. She vaguely heard him call her name, but without looking round, she stepped through the opening and fled down the passageway, the door clanging shut like a death knell behind her.

～

Tristan cursed as he walked back towards the kitchens. What the devil had possessed him? It seemed to be a question he was asking more and more frequently when it came to Roseanna Atwood.

He now knew who her father was, but it was no comfort really. What was the likelihood of a viscount accepting an offer from a French orphan – even if he did have a bloody house in Torquay.

Abruptly, Tris found himself chuckling. What a bacon brain. He cringed, thinking back to his words. Clearly, his verbal intimacy needed practice.

But would she entertain *any* kind of intimacy when this was over? Perhaps she thought him a cad of the highest order, and in truth, his actions had been inexcusable.

God's teeth, now was not the time to be agonising over a woman. The problem was, no matter how many times he told himself that, still she occupied his thoughts, almost to the exclusion of all else. For the first time in his life, he'd found himself imagining what it would be like to have a wife and a family. He might own a house, but in truth, he'd hardly spent any time there. What was the point in him rattling round an empty mausoleum alone?

Sighing, he pushed open the kitchen door and was immediately assailed by the hot, steamy air. The room was bustling, though doubtless things would be far worse after the King arrived.

"Ows 'is ludship settlin' in?' Mrs Higgins asked him in between directing the kitchen staff from her chair. She reminded him of a conductor with his orchestra. Tristan fought the urge to chuckle.

'He seems comfortable enough. I left him putting the finishing touches to his hair. Apparently, my touch is not quite deft enough when it comes to creating a *Brutus*.'

Mrs Higgins gave a hearty laugh, slapping her thigh. 'Lawks, these toffs,' she chortled. 'I bin 'ere fer thirty years, an' they never change. I'm jus' glad the Duke ain't got the same airs and graces.'

Tristan nodded with a grin of his own. 'I'm returning upstairs to put his nibs' clothes away and turn down his bed. I'll be back as soon as I'm finished.'

Although the plan had been for him to try to gain d'Ansouis' trust over four days, they clearly no longer had that luxury, so it had fallen to Tristan to be a little more obvious in his disgruntled servant act – but not so much as to arouse suspicion. A fine line indeed.

The first few minutes of the Comte's arrival as Tristan had shown him to his room had been particularly nerve-wracking. Although Tris had changed beyond measure, there had always been an outside chance that the real Babin would recognise a fellow inmate of Mont Saint Michel. Fortunately, there hadn't been even the slightest flicker of recognition in the bogus Comte's eyes.

But though Tris had prattled on about the state of the nation, d'Ansouis hadn't taken the bait. Indeed, his lordship had spoken very little, and when he did, his tone was guarded and clipped. Hardly surprising given that the bastard was likely preoccupied planning his assassination attempt. The only change had come when he confided the news about the King. The Comte's surprise had been genuine, and when Tristan had daringly shared his opinion of the monarchy, d'Ansouis had regarded him thoughtfully. It was shortly after that he'd been dismissed.

At which point, of course, he should have been reporting back to the Duke, not kissing one of his grace's relatives in the kitchen garden. Tristan sighed. In truth, Nicholas Sinclair would only expect to see him when he had something to report.

Naturally, he intended to search the Comte's bedchamber while d'Ansouis was at dinner, though the chances of the nobleman being foolish enough to leave some incriminating evidence lying around were slim.

Tristan was all too conscious that they were running out of time.

# Nineteen

If Roseanna was flushed and breathless when she arrived in the large drawing room, the only person who remarked upon it was her mother who mentioned how well she was looking. 'Clearly, spending a little more time outdoors is doing you good, darling.'

Rosie felt herself redden further as images of exactly what she'd been doing outdoors not half an hour earlier assailed her. 'Has the Comte come downstairs yet?' she asked, as much to change the subject as a morbid curiosity to finally discover what the rogue looked like.

'He's over there with Grace and Temperance,' Hope responded with a small shudder. 'I must admit I admire their aplomb, but rather them than me. And certainly not you or Frankie. Nicholas was quite right in ordering all of you to stay well away from him wherever possible.'

'I have no wish to converse with the man,' Rosie assured her as they were joined by Francesca, Henrietta and Lilyanna.

While her mother determinedly steered the conversation to more mundane matters, Rosie looked around for Dougal. He was the only one who could say for sure if the man they'd seen earlier today had indeed been Pierre d'Ansouis. At first, she thought the Scot had decided to take dinner in his room, but she finally caught sight of him in conversation with her grandparents. 'If you'll excuse me, I think I will go over and pay my respects to Grandpapa and Grandmama,' she interrupted at the first pause in the conversation, only to fight an unseemly giggle at the four incredulous looks she received in return.

Keeping to the edge of the room to avoid being waylaid by other family members, she quickly reached her destination.

'Have you brought any of that baggage with you?' her grandmother was asking Dougal. 'I must admit I did become rather partial to boiled baggage while I was in Scotland. Very tasty with a bit of turnip.'

'Hello, Grandmama,' Rosie hastily interjected before the old Scot had the opportunity to think up a scathing retort. 'I think you might be referring to haggis.'

'Oh, I can't remember having any of that,' Agnes returned with a frown as Roseanna dutifully kissed her plump cheek.

'If I were you, I'd stop right there,' her grandfather muttered to Rosie. 'Believe me, girl, you'll tie yourself in knots if you continue that conversation.'

Rosie nodded in relief. 'How is your toe, Mr Galbraith?' she asked instead.

'Ah think in the circumstances ye'd better call me Dougal,' he answered. 'Ah think since ah felt oot o' a tree practically on tae yer head, we're well past all the niceties. An' ma toe is still attached tae ma foot, thank ye for askin''

Rosie laughed. Truly, the man was incorrigible.

'Have you spoken to Uncle Nicholas since we returned this afternoon?' she asked her grandfather, wondering if he'd been informed of the latest disastrous developments.

'The Duke asked me tae enlighten him,' Dougal responded. At Rosie's sceptical look, he chortled and added, 'Aye, it took me by surprise an aw. Ah were lookin' fer the flyin' pigs o'er his head.'

'Is our newest guest the same gentleman we met earlier?' Roseanna asked carefully.

'Aye, nae doot aboot it,' Dougal answered. 'Ah told the laird and since then ah've bin keepin' ma distance jest in case he happened tae catch sight o' me.'

'And one look at your physog is likely to be permanently engraved on anybody's brain,' the Reverend retorted.

Dougal gave a delighted guffaw. 'Ah cannae deny ye be improvin', Augustus,' he chuckled.

Reverend Shackleford's lips quirked, though he hurriedly coughed to cover it up. 'Did you tell the Duke about the cull you saw?' he asked Rosie

She nodded, repeating the description she'd given to her uncle and Malcolm earlier as well as the Duke's warning about taking matters into their own hands. Not that she thought that would make any difference to her grandfather.

A gong sounded by the door. 'Dinner is served, your graces,' Mrs Tenner intoned, her curtsy a little deeper than usual. Rosie suspected she was practising for the King.

'I'll prepare you a tincture for your toe, Mr Galbraith,' Agnes suddenly announced as she took the Reverend's arm, 'and Mrs Tomlinson has an excellent knife if it needs to come off.'

∽

Having been furnished with a description of at least one of d'Ansouis' flunkies, Tristan was tempted to go looking once he'd finished searching the Comte's room. The problem was that by then it would be full dark and the possibility of being jumped upon couldn't entirely be discounted. Even if he was merely spotted being somewhere he shouldn't, the conspirators might well grow suspicious. So, as frustrating as it was to have his hands hogtied by being undercover, he knew his best chance of helping bring his old nemesis to justice was by keeping in character. At least for the moment.

Going up the servants' stairs, he headed for the Comte's bedchamber, making sure to carry a couple of extra candles in his pocket. Once outside the room, he knocked loudly, waiting until he was certain there was no one inside.

After a couple of minutes, he pushed open the door and stepped inside.

The room was exactly as he'd left it, but this time there was the faintest trace of an odd smell. It was strange that he'd not noticed it earlier, but then the Comte hadn't exactly been sparing with his hair pomade. Frowning, Tristan remained still, sniffing the stale air. The smell might be faint but even so, it reminded him of something.

He went over to the large dressing table and pulled out the top drawer. A quick search confirmed that nothing had changed since he'd unpacked for the Comte earlier. The other two drawers were the same.

Next, he went over to the tallboy. As soon as he pulled open the first drawer, the smell wafted up to his nose, stronger this time – musty and sulphuric. He recognised it instantly.

Unused gunpowder.

Tristan realised that the reason he hadn't smelled it when he'd unpacked earlier was simply because it hadn't been there. He carefully went through each of the drawers, expecting to find a hidden pistol, but there was nothing untoward in any of them, though the smell gradually became stronger as he got closer to the floor. When he reached the bottom drawer with no luck, he sat back on his heels, baffled.

Maybe d'Ansouis had taken the pistol with him, but it certainly went against all rules of etiquette to carry a weapon into dinner. And even if the Comte intended it to be used to commit murder, it was unlikely he'd be the one doing the firing. So, that left the possibility that he'd hidden the pistol elsewhere for one of his followers to find. If so, when did they intend to use it? And he had no way of knowing whether there was only one.

Swearing in frustration, he pushed the bottom drawer back in with unnecessary force, except that halfway in, it appeared stuck. Gritting his teeth, Tristan pulled it back out, then tried again. This time he was able to push it almost all the way in. 'Third one's a charm,' he muttered to himself, yanking the drawer back out, then shoving it hard. To his relief, it slid back fully. But seconds later the front panel below the drawer fell out.

*

To Rosie's relief, the dinner passed without incident. Indeed, it was quite a lively affair with the Comte d'Ansouis providing many amusing anecdotes of his childhood in France.

The Duke and Duchess were careful to keep any more intimate conversations confined to themselves and the Earl and Countess of Ravenstone. It was perfectly credible, as Adam and Temperance were possessed of the highest rank with the exception of the Marquess of Guildford. However, allowing Patience to exchange more than a couple of sentences with the Comte was entirely out of the question.

The Earl and Countess of Cottesmore provided the additional blockade, effectively preventing any other more imprudent members of the family from getting anywhere near their murderous guest.

Under normal circumstances, of course, the Duchess would have been seated at the opposite end of the table to the Duke, and indeed, that would undoubtedly be the case once the King and the other guests arrived, but tonight the excuse was to ensure the Comte felt at ease as the only non-family member there.

Roseanna had been particularly abstracted during the meal, but since that was nothing out of the ordinary, Frankie, Henri and Lily, thought little of it. Of course, had they known the truth, the three women would not have been nearly so sanguine - after they'd lifted their jaws off the floor naturally.

In truth, Rosie could not stop thinking about Tristan Bernart. Their kiss had unleashed emotions she never even dreamed she possessed. Her mind kept picturing the way he'd pressed her to him - and the way she'd responded. Wantonly thrusting her hips against his hardness. How the devil had she known what to do? She was completely baffled by all of it. Only two things were uppermost in her mind.

Firstly, she wanted to do it again – the sooner the better, and secondly, he'd told her he had a house in Torquay.

He would not have shared that with her if all he'd wanted from her was a quick tumble.

~

The smell of musty sulphur became suddenly stronger, and Tristan laid his head on the floor and pushed his hand into the aperture. After a second, his fingers touched what felt like cloth. Grasping it between his thumb and forefinger, he dragged it towards him, finally pulling out a white shirt. Except there was hardly any white left on it.

Frowning, Tristan climbed to his feet and held out the shirt. The fine lawn was liberally coated in what looked like fine black dust which was clearly the source of the smell.

He'd been wrong, the black powder hadn't come from a pistol. There was far too much of it for that to be the case. Tristan froze as he realised the truth.

This much powder had to have come from a barrel. And a barrel of black powder would only be used for one thing.

An explosion.

Tristan felt himself come out in a cold sweat. On its own, one barrel of black powder could certainly do some damage, but it would be localised. He didn't know what Babin's ultimate objective was, but causing as much chaos as possible had to be a priority.

Blowing up the house of a prominent member of the aristocracy whilst the heads of the two major political parties were in residence would certainly fit the bill. And now, by some unlucky coincidence, the King of England would also be present...

Tristan felt sick. To achieve the damage Babin was looking for, he would certainly need more than one barrel of black powder. All of them placed strategically to create the most impact.

That was why the bastard needed a plan of the house.

# Twenty

The mood in the Duke's study the next morning was sober to say the least.

The King was due to arrive late in the afternoon, well in time to attend the evening's entertainment. Wellington and Grey too would be present, along with the twenty-two other guests invited for the weekend. This evening's dinner had been planned as an amusing introduction to the weekend's diversions. Afterwards, there was to be dancing and games.

For an anarchist, what better time to ignite an explosion?

Nicholas had called together all of his brothers-in-law. However, on this occasion, he'd deliberately kept their wives in the dark. Including Grace. He would rather deal with her anger than her lifeless corpse when all this was over, and he well knew how fear could turn a difficult situation into a bloodbath.

'The mistake we made was in assuming that the Comte d'Ansouis would not do anything precipitous whilst a guest in the same house, but clearly, he had a plan in place to ensure he was well away before any explosion occurred.' Nicholas's voice was grim.

'He wouldn't need to escape,' Jago stated flatly. 'All he'd need to do was make sure he was nowhere near the blast area when the explosion occurred. Retiring to his bedchamber with a feigned illness would likely be enough.'

'No doubt returning to help the wounded with nobody the wiser,' Christian grated. 'Can we not just arrest the bastard now?'

Jamie shook his head. 'We have no proof aside from a soiled shirt which Tristan has had to replace to hide the fact that we're on to him. If we give him any reason to run, it won't help us find the other conspirators. And d'Ansouis was never going to be the one lighting the fuse. We don't even know how many more there are.'

'Our best option is to find the powder and render it harmless before this evening.'

'And how exactly do we do that?' Anthony asked, his voice carefully controlled.

'He wants tonight to be a bloodbath,' Nicholas predicted. 'The only time he can guarantee that every guest will be present is during dinner. My guess is that the black powder has been positioned somewhere in the cellars directly underneath the dining room.'

'The last I looked, those cellars were filled tae bursting wi' barrels containing everything from salt beef, to…'

'Gunpowder,' Adam supplied drily.

'Aye,' Malcolm nodded. 'We're nae goin' tae simply walk in there and find them.'

'And we don't want to scare off the conspirators,' Gabriel added. 'Catching them in the act is the only way we'll ever be able to identify them. Especially since we don't know how many there are.'

'And unless d'Ansouis makes a mistake to unmask himself, the only way we'll see the bastard swing is if they give him up,' Tristan added.

'I'd like to know how the devil they managed to sneak the barrels into the cellar in the first place,' Max put in, speaking for the first time. 'It can't have been easy. They must have a contact inside the house.'

'It wouldnae have been that difficult,' Malcolm countered. 'There have been so many deliveries in the last few days. But I agree wi' ye, they likely have a contact working inside the house.'

'I think most of you are aware that I have a small team of ex naval men on standby for when the family needs extra protection,' Nicholas declared. 'Their team leader is a man named Chapman. I'm expecting them to arrive before noon, so there will be six more footmen on duty by early afternoon. I called them in yesterday to provide extra protection for his majesty and our two politicians, but given what Tristan discovered, I think they will be best utilised to neutralise the threat in the cellar once we've discovered the whereabouts of the gunpowder.'

'So, they'll be the ones waiting for the murdering varmints to turn up and try to light the fuses?' Adam queried.

'Aye, they'll give the bastards a surprise they weren't expecting.' Malcolm's grin was fierce.

Nicholas gave a humourless chuckle. 'So, gentlemen, the job for today is to somehow find the right barrels hidden in a cellar filled with lots of other barrels, without anyone knowing they've been discovered. Then they are to be quietly diffused, moved out of harm's way and replaced with barrels containing something else – preferably non-flammable. After that, our men wait for the murdering varmints to turn up and try to light the fuses, when they either shoot them or send them for the morning drop.'

'Have I covered it all?'

~

Unusually, Roseanna did not wake until the maid came in with her morning chocolate. Since Trixie had come into her life, she'd rarely slept past eight o'clock. While the chamber maid bustled about, opening curtains and placing a fresh bowl of washing water on the dressing table,

Rosie endeavoured to collect herself, only half listening to the young woman's chatter.

'I still can't believe 'is 'ighenss is goin' to be at Blackmore today,' she declared, her voice radiating delight. 'It just don't seem real. I reckon I'll remember this day for as long as I live.'

Rosie smiled at the maid's enthusiasm but struggled to feel even the smallest excitement. After tossing and turning for what seemed like hours, her mind relentlessly fluctuating between exhilaration and fear, she envied the maid her ignorance.

She desperately wanted to speak with Tristan. Their kiss the night before had turned her world upside down, but had it done the same for him? The way he'd taken control suggested he'd done it many times before, but somehow, she'd sensed that what they'd shared had been an unfamiliar experience for him, too. While part of her was petrified of what might happen in the hours to come, another part was equally frightened of what might happen after it was all over. Or rather, what might not.

How could she return to Northwood pretending nothing had happened and act like nothing had changed? *Everything* had changed. And her twin sister – the one person she'd always shared all her secrets with, wasn't even aware of it.

Sighing, Rosie pushed back the coverlet and climbed out of bed. Trixie eyed her sleepily but didn't appear in any hurry to move. Rosie bent to stroke her soft ears. 'As much as I'd like to stay here with you for the rest of the day, it won't solve anything,' she murmured, kissing the top of the little dog's head. 'and there are other, much more important things to be concerned about than my heart.'

'Like everybody surviving the day.'

To Roseanna's relief, the Comte did not appear for breakfast, but then, neither did her father or any of her uncles. When she questioned the Duchess, her aunt replied that there were things that needed taking care of before the King's arrival. And since she too had a million and one things to supervise, she would leave them to their own devices.

Jennifer suggested that since the guests were not due to start arriving until later in the afternoon, they take the dogs on a walk to Wistman's pool. Initially Roseanna thought to decline, but then thought better of it. She'd spent very little time with her cousins, and what was she going to do if she remained in the house? Brooding and getting under the busy servants' feet wouldn't help anything. And anyway, Trixie would enjoy spending some time with her canine cousins.

'Do you think your father would like to accompany us?' she asked Brendon.

'Ah dinnae ken,' the Scot answered. 'He put more than a wee dent in his grace's whisky supply last evenin' and will likely be nursin' a sore head fer his sins.'

'He didn't say anything to the Comte while he was foxed did he?' Rosie asked anxiously.

'Nae, ma lady dinnae ye worry. The old bampot didnae hae a chance. His lordship retired not long after ye, an' ah told the Reverend ah'd be sure tae put the daftie in his bed maself.'

Roseanna couldn't help but giggle at Brendon's description of his father. While his frustration was evident, so was the affection in his voice.

'Did my grandfather say he'd be coming over to the house today?'

'Aye, ah reckon he's resigned himself tae bein' stuck tae ma da's hip until the weekend's be done. Ah'm beyond grateful tae the pair o' ye.'

Everyone going agreed to meet outside the stables at ten. If they didn't dawdle, the walk to Wistman's pool and back would likely take them a pair of hours. According to Patience, stout boots were definitely required.

There was no sign of Tristan or any of the other men as Roseanna returned to her bedchamber to collect Trixie and change into her walking boots. She only hoped they managed to track down the conspirators before the scoundrels had the opportunity to shoot anybody. Although, what would happen to the Comte then, she had no idea.

Picking up her shawl, she wondered if Dougal would accompany them to the pool. The thought of the old Scot being left to his own devices for any amount of time was still not a comforting one - especially if the last evening was anything to go by...

Clearly, they could not all go down and search the cellars en masse. If they did, it would surely be noticed. Instead, it was decided that all of them bar Nicholas, Malcolm and Tristan would go down in pairs disguised as kitchen staff. With organised chaos currently prevailing in Mrs Higgins' domain, it was unlikely their deception would be discovered, and with the sheer number of deliveries even now being received, their anonymity would be all but assured.

Unfortunately, while Nicholas and Malcolm were the two most familiar with the layout of the extensive cellars, they were also the two with the most recognisable faces. And the Duke of Blackmore especially would not under any circumstances be seen rummaging around in his cellars.

Instead, the Duke had furnished them with a plan of the cellars, marking the three areas underneath the large dining room, while he and Malcolm went to prepare for a visit from the King.

Etienne Babin paced back and forth in his bedchamber. In truth, he couldn't remain still. It was difficult to actually believe all the years of plotting and scheming were finally about to bear fruit.

Blackmore hadn't been the only house he'd planted *Revisionists* in. Some had been in place for years. There was never any shortage of servants ready to betray their masters, and the English loved to whine.

But it hadn't been until his invitation to the Duke of Blackmore's annual garden party that he finally saw the opportunity he'd been waiting for. And the discovery that Wellington and Grey were to be present was an unexpected stroke of luck. Everything had gone to plan, right down to locating an old drawing of the cellars, and setting the casks in place without attracting attention.

Everything that is, apart from the discovery that the bloody King was coming. When Babin had first been told, he could hardly believe it. It felt like divine providence – a gift from on high.

But gradually, throughout the night, unease had set in. It was one thing blowing up politicians and entitled peers, but it was quite another to assassinate Royalty. If he was caught and found guilty, he could very well be hung, drawn and quartered. *Merde*, the English were barbarians.

But the dice had been thrown, and the game was on. It was too late to back out now. And still he relished the thought of the chaos the act would bring. He just didn't want to have to watch his own entrails burning as a result of it.

He'd intended to brazen it out, confident he'd be accepted as one of the victims, but

the more he thought about it, the more he realised that the only sensible action would be to flee across the Channel.

He had contacts in Plymouth and was confident he'd be able to secure passage quite easily.

His problem was more immediate. How would he get to the docks? If he took his coach, everyone would know he'd left. Questions could be asked that might lead to his arrest before he reached France. If he feigned illness, however, he could simply leave the house with none the wiser. With luck they might even believe he'd perished in the blast.

He was certain there'd be someone in the village with a horse and cart who'd be willing to take him to Plymouth for the right price. And if the man was unfortunate enough to meet with an accident before he had the chance to return to Blackmore...

Babin looked down at his pocket watch. It was nearly nine a.m., which meant the maid would be in shortly. If he was leaving, it would have to be as soon as she'd finished.

His mind made up, the false Comte sat down to write a note.

~

Although Nicholas had provided a detailed plan of the cellars, in reality, the number of small, vaulted rooms in each section numbered more than ten. And nearly all of them were completely filled with barrels. Whilst brandy and port were easily identifiable by their pungent aroma, they also masked the subtler smell of sulphur, forcing the men to pull out and go through each individual barrel in turn.

As the owner of a Cornish tin mine, Jago had the most experience when it came to quantities of powder needed to blow up a specific area. In his opinion, the amount of black powder needed to produce a blast large enough to devastate the dining room and everyone in it would be between ten and twelve barrels - stacked together to cause the maximum amount of damage. Since the barrels were likely only about two feet tall, by a foot across, they could quite easily be hidden away behind the larger casks.

After an hour, they swapped, with the outgoing pair bringing up a cask of something to foster the impression they'd been sent to fetch provisions for the kitchen. A chalk mark was made next to the entrance once they were certain an area was safe.

It was laborious and time consuming to check every barrel in each of the small rooms and after two hours, Adam, Roan, Christian and Anthony - the first two pairs – had only managed to search half the area underneath the dining room. All eight men were acutely aware they were running out of time.

~

Tristan had to fight his frustration at having to remain on call for the Comte, but it was crucial they maintain the deception at this stage in the game. The Frenchman had sent a note down that he was not to be disturbed. Apparently, he was sick with an ague and wished to remain in bed to protect his majesty's person. In reality, the scab was undoubtedly hiding away until after the dining room had gone up in flames, at which point he'd simply claim to be another victim.

In all honesty, Tristan didn't know how he'd stop himself from strangling the former convict with his own cravat when he finally went upstairs, but he gritted his teeth and resigned himself to watching and waiting.

∽

It was a long time since Dougal Galbraith had felt quite so shabby. As a younger man, he'd prided himself on his ability to drink a bottle of whisky and still walk out on his own two feet.

Sadly, if the last evening was anything to go by, he appeared to have lost that ability, especially since he couldn't actually remember how he'd got to bed. He blamed it on being surrounded by a bunch of lily-livered Sassenachs. But gutless or no, he couldn't deny that the Duke of Blackmore had in his possession a very fine whisky indeed. And experience told him that on occasions like these, the only thing for it was to have another wee dram.

The problem was, it had taken him nearly half an hour to negotiate the stairs and find his way back to the drawing room, only to discover the bloody decanter was empty.

Sighing, he sat down on a chair and wondered what to do now. Perhaps he should have gone for a walk with Brendon and the others. A bit of fresh air would probably have done him good. He looked dubiously out of the window, wincing at the bright sunlight

A small stroll in the fresh air – that was what he needed. And if it happened to take him past his grace's cellar – particularly the one where he kept his whisky – well, then that would be a fortunate coincidence.

∽

Rosie enjoyed the walk much more than she expected to, and for a while, it was lovely to put her concerns to one side and simply enjoy her extended family's company. Spending this time with her aunts and cousins, and watching her mother interact with her sisters, had been unexpectedly wonderful – despite all the havey-cavey business surrounding them.

As they came within sight of the house, Roseanna couldn't help noticing that everyone's steps had become unmistakeably slower as concerns about the current situation came flooding back.

Under normal circumstances, they would undoubtedly be sharing their excitement about the coming royal visit, but during their hike, it had hardly been mentioned and as they descended towards the stables, the only comment made was concerning royal etiquette.

By the time they reached the grain store, they were all largely silent. James helped little Henry down off his shoulders. Lunch would be a very improvised affair, as the kitchen would be entirely focused on the evening's dinner.

'Will the Comte be joining us for lunch do you think?' Rosie asked no one in particular.

'I deuced well hope not,' Patience responded. 'Being the slippery toad he is, my guess is he'll remain in his bedchamber, plotting, until the King arrives.'

'If he does join us, we'll have to be civil,' Prudence commented, 'even if what we'd really like to do is to run the blackguard through.'

'You've never been civil to anyone in your life that you didn't like,' Charity scoffed.

'That's not true. I'm *particularly* civil to people I don't like,' Pru countered with a grin.

A few minutes later, they parted to freshen up for lunch.

Putting Trixie back on her lead, Rosie was about to follow her sister when a figure coming out of the carriage house caught her eye. Stopping, she squinted, making out the grey hair tied back in a queue. It was the man she'd seen at the inn. She watched him talk with an unknown man for a second, not sure what to do. 'Are you coming, Rosie?' Her sister's question decided her.

'You go on without me. I think Trixie might need to do her business.'

'How can she possibly have any business left to do after spending the entire morning outdoors?' Francesca queried. 'Truly, I think that little madam has you wrapped around her paw.'

Roseanna found herself chuckling as she caught up. She couldn't really argue with her sister's comment.

'I'll see you at lunch,' she murmured, giving Francesca a quick hug. Her twin gave the smallest of frowns as she stepped away. 'I think there is something you're not telling me, Rosie,' she declared. 'And while I will not badger you into confiding, neither will I let the matter drop. Be warned, dearest.'

Knowing her sister's doggedness of old, Roseanna stood for a second, watching her walk away. It was actually quite a comfort to know that she had someone who knew her almost as well as she knew herself.

Then she turned towards her quarry just as he finished his conversation. She'd have to hurry if she wanted to see where he was going.

Picking up her skirts, she hurried towards the carriage house. Unfortunately, by the time she got there, he'd disappeared. 'Damn,' she murmured to herself, turning full circle. There was no sign of him. She was just about to give up when she saw Dougal Galbraith walking along the edge of the kitchen garden. Where was her grandfather? Surely, he should have been here by now.

Biting her bottom lip, Rosie hesitated. Did she keep looking for the possible traitor, or follow Dougal to make sure he wasn't up to anything untoward? She bent down to pick Trixie up. Her uncle had expressly forbidden her to go after the grey-haired man if she ever saw him again, and Rosie was convinced that the mischief Dougal could cause was in no way diminished because they happened to be in the middle of a crisis, despite what everyone else seemed to think – well, everyone but her grandfather. But where the devil was he?

## Twenty-One

Augustus Shackleford could not imagine what had possessed him when he'd decided to walk to Blackmore. It had only been twenty minutes, but he was already hot and bothered and, what's more, he was unlikely to arrive in time for lunch. He could only hope he didn't arrive at the same time as the King. In truth, he should already have been keeping a watchful eye on Dougal, but he'd been unable to resist sharing the news with Percy that his majesty was coming to Blackmore.

Given the tense circumstances, Nicholas had been careful to keep the impromptu visit a secret. Indeed, the Reverend had yet to share the news with Agnes. He'd be lucky to escape with his ballocks intact once she found out. But the clergyman knew he could safely rely on Percy to keep the visit between himself and Lizzy. With luck, Finn would get to meet the King of England at the Garden Party tomorrow.

Providing that things didn't go to hell in a handcart before then of course...

He was just about to pass the old tithe barn on the edge of the village when he caught sight of two men standing in a patch of shadow. He wouldn't have paid them much attention except that Flossy began a low grumbling. The sound she made when she really didn't like someone.

Over the years, Reverend Shackleford had come to trust the little dog's instincts. Flossy knew a blackguard when she saw one. Instinctively, the clergyman quickened his steps, but to his surprise, Flossy held back, her lip curling back over her teeth. The Reverend slowed and looked back. From this angle, he could see the men clearly and he drew a sharp breath in surprise. One of them was the Comte d'Ansouis.

∽

Tristan Bernart stared at the Comte's empty bedchamber. Had Babin done a runner? If so, he'd left all his clothes and belongings. And to leave now made no sense. The only way he could hope to evade the noose was to pretend to be one of the victims of the explosion. If he ran now, fingers would point straight at him.

Unless, of course, he intended to escape to France.

Perhaps that had been his intention all along. To set everything up, then escape before Blackmore went up in flames.

Or perhaps his decision had been a hasty one. Up until his arrival, he'd did not know his majesty would be present. To kill the King might well be every revolutionary's dream, but it set the stakes infinitely higher. If he was caught, he'd face far worse than the morning drop.

Tristan gritted his teeth, wondering exactly when the bastard had left. It could have been hours ago. And he'd been waiting for the bell to ring like a good little valet. It was only as lunch approached that he decided to ignore the Comte's instructions not to be disturbed.

Some bloody conspirator he'd make.

Swearing under his breath, he went down to tell the Duke.

∽

At first, Roseanna couldn't fathom where the old Scot was going. He didn't seem to have any destination in mind, but she supposed it wasn't beyond the realm of possibility that he was simply going for a stroll.

Perhaps she should tell him that lunch would be served in less than half an hour.

She quickened her pace, intending to ask if he wished to accompany her, but before she could get close enough to hail him, he promptly disappeared. For a second her steps faltered, then she picked up her pace again, fearing he'd fallen. The last thing the poor man needed was a broken leg to go with his toe.

Seconds later, she arrived at the place Dougal had vanished. It was an open courtyard, one that she'd never been in before. The laundry room and scullery were to the right and, looking around, she could see a couple of empty carts like the one the two conspirators had been in the day before. However, the courtyard was currently deserted, although she could hear voices coming from the laundry room.

She took a few steps forward and spun round. There was no sign of the old Scot. Turning back towards the house, she suddenly spotted a set of steps leading downwards. From her position, she could just see the top of a door.

Putting Trixie down on the ground, she walked towards the steps. As she got closer, she realised she was looking at Blackmore's cellars, and the door was wide open.

∽

Picking Flossy up to stop her grumbling, the Reverend stepped to the side of the barn where he couldn't be seen. Once the little dog was quiet, he was able to hear what was being said.

'Mary said yer wantin' a lift to Plymouth. It'll be ten bob, an' not a penny less.'

The Reverend couldn't help wincing. Ten shillings? He was being robbed. Wait 'til the varmint saw the state of the old Alf's cart. He'd be lucky to reach Plymouth by Christmas. And why the devil was he going to Plymouth anyway?

To the clergyman's surprise, the Comte accepted the cost without quibbling.

'It'll tek me 'alf an hour to catch Dolly 'an 'itch 'er to the wagon,' Alf went on.

'Can't you get here any sooner?' There was both frustration and fear in the Frenchman's growl.

'You could always walk,' was Alf's matter-of-fact response. 'Best wait inside the barn. This 'eat ain't good fer a nob.'

Seconds later Alf strolled unhurriedly back towards the village, whistling, while his would-be passenger stood watching with gritted teeth. After a few moments, however, the Comte picked up his valise, pulled opened the door and stepped into the dimness of the tithe barn. Given that the barn was a haven for rats and smelled like it, the Reverend guessed he was more concerned about being seen than avoiding a suntan.

Evidently the Frog was doing a runner. The Reverend had no idea what the implications of that might be, but he knew he had to stop Pierre d'Ansouis from leaving Blackmore - and he only had half an hour to do it. Obviously, he could pay Alf the ten shillings not to take the Comte, but the old skinflint would likely ask for eleven instead.

He needed Percy.

~

'We've searched the whole of the area directly underneath the dining room and found nothing.' Adam's frustration was clear. 'Could we have got it wrong?'

The two men were conferring in the Duke's study as usual, though Adam had barely recognised his friend. Nicholas rarely dressed so ostentatiously.

'It's more likely they did,' the Duke responded. They weren't able to access the most current plan of the cellars, and the one they lost to Rosie wasn't entirely accurate, so it could be they managed to unearth one that was even older - before the most recent alterations were made to the house.'

'Fiend seize it, it'll take us hours to check every bloody cellar,' Adam grated.

'Where are the others?' Nicholas quizzed him.

'In the laundry room.' The Earl gave a weary grin before adding, 'Fortunately, one of the barrels we brought back up contained a side of salt pork, so at least we won't go hungry.'

A sudden knock interrupted their conversation. Directing Adam out of sight, Nicholas opened the door to a thunderous Tristan.

'You'd better come in.' Nicholas couldn't imagine what the hell had gone wrong now.

Tristan strode in, his body tense with anger. 'Our charlatan Comte has done a runner,' he announced through gritted teeth.

The other two men stared at him in silence for a brief second. 'Are you certain?' Nicholas didn't waste time asking how Tristan knew, accepting his nod at face value.

'We have no choice but to continue on regardless,' the Duke growled. 'We have to assume he planned this, leaving the other conspirators to finish what he started.'

'Continue looking,' he ordered Adam, 'We have to have found the powder by the time the King arrives. Since you can't find it under the dining room, it may be that they don't intend to wait until dinner.'

'My gut is telling me that Babin didn't plan this,' Tristan stated flatly. 'I think he got cold feet at the thought of what might happen if he's caught with the King's blood on his hands.'

'If that's the case, then his flunkies are probably not aware that he's gone,' Adam pointed out. 'When they find out, the carefully timed plan could well go out of the window. Has Chapman arrived yet?'

Nicholas shook his head. 'Go back upstairs and search the bastard's room, Tris,' he instructed, 'and report back anything you find that we don't already know.'

～

Roseanna went down the steps and peeked through the door. The small, vaulted room was dark, but from the light shining in through the doorway, she could see the outlines of what looked like barrels stacked from floor to ceiling. Down the middle was a clear path. Why on earth would Dougal come down here all on his own? Clearly, he wasn't concerned about being alone in the dark.

'Mr Galbraith,' she called softly, 'Dougal – are you in here?' Her voice echoed off the arched ceiling, but there was no answer. Roseanna bit her lip uncertainly. She had no idea what to do. If Dougal had come down here willingly, then mayhap she should just leave him to it.

But what if he hurt himself? 'Damn and blast,' she muttered under her breath. She looked down at Trixie. The little dog was sniffing round the closest barrels, seemingly unconcerned by the lack of light. Gritting her teeth, Rosie turned back and pushed the door open as far as it would go, then she took one step forward, followed by another, one hand holding Trixie's lead and the other stretched out in front of her as she waited for her eyes to get used to the dimness. After about three feet or so, the little dog trotted past her, pulling on the lead.

Surprised, Rosie followed, stepping through an archway into the next vaulted room. To her relief, there was a lighted lantern hanging from the ceiling. She began to realise that the cellars comprised a series of identical vaulted rooms, each one with domed apertures positioned around the edge, leaving a clear path through the middle. From what she could see, nearly every aperture was filled with barrels.

Trixie trotted on purposefully, and not knowing what else to do, Roseanna followed. As she stepped through the archway to the next room, she began to hear a rhythmic knocking sound. Suddenly afraid, she stopped dead and listened - it sounded like someone was tapping something.

Abruptly deciding she'd had enough, Rosie bent down, intending to pick Trixie up and retrace her steps. However, the little dog had other ideas. As soon as the lead went slack, she pulled hard, jerking the handle out of her mistress's hand. Then she shot off, her tail wagging madly. 'Trixie!' Rosie ran after her, completely disregarding her earlier attempt at silence.

The tapping stopped, then a familiar voice said, 'Ah ken ye smelled the whisky, Beatrix. Ye be a bonny wee lass after ma own heart. Dinnae fash yersel, ah willnae be long. Ah reckon a couple more taps should dae it.'

Roseanna finally caught sight of Dougal Galbraith on his knees, using a flat stone to tap a thin sliver of wood into the crack underneath the barrel's seal. He was surrounded by four open casks.

'What on earth are you doing, Dougal?' she gasped.

'It took me a while, but ma nose never fails me,' the Scot answered cheerfully, without stopping. Seconds later, the seal popped off and the pungent aroma of malt whisky filled the air. 'Ha Ha,' he crowed, climbing to his feet. 'Dae ye fancy a wee dram, ma lady?'

'Dougal, what the deuce are you doing, stealing the Duke's whisky?' Rosie gasped, horrified. 'And why are there all these opened barrels?'

'Ah kenned it be here,' Dougal answered with a chuckle. 'Ah jest haed a few false starts.' He looked round at the open casks. 'Ah dinnae ken what be in 'em, but the smell reminds me o' when ah've had too many neeps wi' ma haggis.'

Frowning, Roseanna stepped over to the nearest barrel. The stink rising from the cask was the same as the one she'd smelled in the cart, only much, much worse. Gagging, she covered her nose. Then she picked up the Scot's abandoned sliver of wood and poked it into the barrel. A small cloud of what looked like black soot billowed up.

Dougal looked over her shoulder. 'Come tae think o' it,' he muttered, 'that looks jest like the pooder Brendon haes in his gun back at Caerlaverock.'

## Twenty-Two

'Right then, Percy, we haven't got much time. Has Lizzy still got that candlestick Grace gave her for Christmas – the one where the cherub's wearing nothing but his smalls?'

Percy looked up in confusion as Reverend Shackleford burst through the front door.

'Come along, Percy, get a grip. I might have negotiated another ten minutes with Alf, but it still gives us less than half an hour to give the varmint a deuced headache before the old skinflint gets back with the cart and the Frog ends up in Plymouth.'

Percy stood up, more bewildered than he'd ever been in his entire life. He wondered if the Reverend had finally become addled.

'What exactly do you want it for, Sir?' he asked carefully, particularly concerned about the reference to a headache.

'No time for that now lad, I'll tell you on the way.'

'Where are we going?' the curate asked, standing his ground.

Augustus Shackleford gave a long-suffering sigh. 'Once again, Percy Noon, we have been called upon to save this fair nation. This time from that bacon-brained Frog who, as it turns out, had plans to murder the King.'

'Then why is he going to Plymouth?'

The Reverend opened his mouth, then closed it again. In truth, the clergyman had no idea whether the Comte had *actually* planned to do away with his majesty, but why else would he be running away if not because someone had cried rope on the blackguard.

He was getting desperate. He gritted his teeth. 'Please, Percy, I really can't do this on my own. I swear I'll do the braining – all you'll have to do is tie the varmint up.'

'With what?'

It had to be said the curate was becoming slightly hysterical. The Reverend wanted to cry. All these years, and Percy was every bit as chuckle headed as he'd always been. Oh, there was that brief time when they'd saved Agnes from having her finger chopped off by George's murderous foster father, but it hadn't lasted long...

Augustus Shackleford gave an inward groan. 'With this.' He held up a length of rope that had just cost him two shillings from that deuced money grubber. At this rate, he'd be in Dun territory by the end of the day.

'Once we have him secured, we'll lock him up in the tithe barn for his grace to deal with...' He paused before adding slyly, 'I'm certain the Duke will want to thank you personally for helping secure a traitor.'

He could see that the curate was wavering. In Percy's eyes, Nicholas Sinclair was only slightly less important than God.

'Swear you won't hit him too hard.'

'I wouldn't dare,' the Reverend answered truthfully. 'I doubt I've got long before I'm scheduled for tea and toast with the Almighty. The last thing I want to do is risk ending up on the end of old Nick's toasting fork instead.'

For a second, Percy looked as if he might cry. Then he squared his shoulders and took Lizzy's candlestick off the mantlepiece. 'Lead on, Sir,' he said with barely a quaver.

'*Belter*. So, what be ma job then?'

~

Roseanna dropped the stick like it was the gun Dougal had referred to. 'This is gunpowder?' she breathed. 'What's it doing here?' She became aware she was standing on what felt like a length of thick yarn.

'Don't move Rosie.' Her father's stern voice came from directly behind her. Roseanna froze, as much from guilt as fear. Then she frowned as he shouted, 'Max, we've found it. Fetch Jago and Jamie.'

Minutes later, Roseanna was surrounded by the four men while Dougal watched with interest from his seat on the now closed whisky barrel, Trixie at his feet.

'Step back carefully, love,' her father ordered her once they'd re-secured the lids on all four barrels.

Swallowing, Rosie stepped backwards until she could no longer feel the rope under her feet.

'If we follow the fuse, we'll find the rest of them,' Jago commented, his voice laced with relief.

'I can't even begin to speculate how both of you came to be here,' Gabriel commented drily, 'but it appears that we owe you our thanks.' He turned to Dougal, who was now attempting to hold his pilfered jug of whisky behind his back. 'Mr Galbraith, I would be grateful if you could please take my daughter and your highly inflammable jug of liqueur far away from these cellars.'

'Dae ye reckon ah be giein a knighthood fer this?' he asked, getting to his feet.

'I wouldn't count on it,' muttered Max from the shadows as he traced the fuse to another six barrels stacked tightly in the corner.

'Go straight to the Duke, Rosie,' Jamie instructed, 'and tell him we've found it.' Roseanna nodded, not knowing whether to laugh or cry as she picked up Trixie and followed Dougal back towards the entrance.

'Mr Galbraith,' Jamie added, raising his voice to ensure it carried to the disappearing Scot. He waited until Dougal stopped and turned round. '*Tell no one.*' The magistrate's final command left absolutely no room for misunderstanding...

*

'Your job will be to look out for Alf's cart,' Reverend Shackleford told Finn as the lad trotted happily behind them. Both he and Percy well knew there was no point in forbidding the boy to accompany them – he'd simply take a different route.

The curate scowled at his superior as they approached the tithe barn. Lizzy would have his hide if any harm came to the boy. Not that he'd be able to live with himself either.

'Right then,' the Reverend hissed as they arrived at the side of the barn, 'you've got the rope, Percy, and I've got the candlestick...'

'Ah reckon if ye grab him where his ballocks be, Revren, ye'll get a much better swing,' Finn interrupted, his whisper deadly serious.

The two men stared at the boy. 'I'm not sure I'm strong enough to grab the fellow's baubles,' the clergyman muttered after a moment.

'Nae *his*, Ah'm talkin aboot the candlestick.' Finn sniggered as he pointed to the cherub's loin cloth.

The Reverend grasped the candlestick round the cupid's nether regions, as the lad had suggested. It was actually the perfect place for him to get a good a swing. He felt a moment's disquiet at the boy's instinctive grasp of such tactics. What had the Almighty got planned for him?

'I'm going to knock on the door,' the clergyman whispered. 'As soon as he opens it, I'll give him a quick tap on the noggin. Then you run in, Percy and truss the blackguard up like a deuced chicken. Are we ready?'

Father and son nodded solemnly and after only a slight hesitation, Reverend Shackleford gave the door a sharp knock.

For a second, it looked as though the Comte had already left the barn, but after a moment there came the sound of a latch lifting. Taking a step backwards, the Reverend readied himself.

But as the Comte opened the door, the Reverend just couldn't do it. What kind of an example was he setting to Finn? Tare an' hounds, he was supposed to be God's representative on earth. He should be upholding His values, not making deuced excuses to break them.

The two men stared at each other for a second. When the Comte spoke, his voice contemptuous. 'Who the devil are you and where's that imbecile with the cart?'

The varmint hadn't recognised him. Reverend Shackleford blinked, completely thrown.

'He be waitin' fer yer roond the corner, yer ludship,' Finn piped up, stepping forward. 'He sent us tae fetch ye.'

The Comte narrowed his eyes for a second, then giving a disdainful nod, picked up his valise and took a step through the doorway, just as an enormous rat came scuttling past his feet. With a horrified yell, the Frenchman lifted his foot, intending to bring it down on the rodent's head.

Flossy had had enough. She'd spent the whole time growling under her breath. As the nobleman lifted his foot, the little dog leapt forward and wrapped her sharp teeth round his ankle. With a scream, the Comte dropped his valise and tried to pedal backwards, but his feet got tangled up in his baggage. Seconds later, his head hit the ground with a loud crack.

'I tek it he ain't goin' to need that ride to Plymouth,' Alf spoke up behind them.

Percy hurried over to the Comte's motionless body and used the rope to secure the nobleman's hands and feet.

'That he isn't,' the Reverend commented cheerfully. 'But I'll give you a shilling to take him back to the Duke.'

∽

By the middle of the afternoon, the King had still not arrived, but the Duke had received word that his majesty was half an hour away. Most of the other guests were already making themselves at home, including the Duke of Wellington and Lord Grey. Naturally, the politicians had been given chambers at opposite ends of the house.

The barrels of black powder had been swapped for the same number of casks containing harmless food stuffs. The fuses had been replaced in exactly the same position and Chapman's men were ready and waiting for the conspirators to show themselves.

To say that Nicholas was surprised at the arrival of the unconscious Comte d'Ansouis would have been putting it mildly. He gave the driver his requested twenty shillings and locked the would-be traitor in Blackmore's one and only dungeon.

When his majesty finally arrived, both the Duke and Duchess were ready and waiting on the steps of Blackmore, and if her grace blanched a little at the number of retainers climbing out of the fleet of carriages, she hid it well.

As Roseanna readied herself for the dinner, she couldn't help thinking about the *Revisionists* still hidden in plain sight amongst Blackmore's staff. After passing her father's message onto the Duke, her uncle had first of all closed his eyes in relief, then had done her the courtesy of relating the events of the last day and a half. But although the danger of an explosion had passed, they still did not know exactly how many conspirators there were, and so far, Etienne Babin was not talking.

Rosie decided to wear her favourite apricot evening gown for dinner. After all, it wasn't often one had the opportunity to dine at the same table as the King of England. And she couldn't discount the possibility that Tristan would get to see her.

In truth, it seemed overly frivolous to be concerned with fripperies whilst danger still lurked, but Roseanna told herself that neglecting to dress her best for dinner certainly wasn't going to change matters one way or another. And it made her feel better.

All members of the family were expected to play hosts to the newly arrived guests, and ordinarily Rosie would have run post haste in the opposite direction at such a request. But the last few days had changed something inside of her. The desire to hide away was not quite so prevalent and she'd found herself actually seeking the company of others.

Leaving Trixie curled up asleep, Roseanna went to call for her sister. Both had been obliged to see to their own hair since available lady's maids were now akin to gold dust. Rosie had opted for a simple twist, though the number of pins securing her hair made her feel like a hedgehog. Francesca too had elected to do a humble chignon and, on their way downstairs, she confided to Roseanna that she feared most of the pins were actually stuck in her head.

Both girls were giggling as they entered the drawing room and for a second Rosie didn't notice Tristan Bernart standing next to the enormous fireplace. When she finally caught sight of him, she stumbled, her heart constricting in her chest. Tonight, he was wearing full evening dress like every other man in the room. Had he shed his servant guise?

Her stare did not go unnoticed by her sister. 'So *that's* what I've been missing,' she mused. 'Roseanna Atwood, when this evening is over, I will not allow you to retire until you have divulged all.' Feeling suddenly light-hearted, Rosie giggled. All of a sudden, anything seemed possible.

She was still giggling as the King entered the room. The ladies performed deep curtsies, and the men bowed. And for the first time ever, Roseanna did not wish she was back in her bedchamber.

In Roseanna's eyes, dinner was a truly magical affair. The conversation sparkled. She sparkled, and all the while Tristan was looking at her as though she was the most precious thing in the world. She was certain his attention had not gone unnoticed by her mother and father, but for once, she didn't care. She was in love for the first time in her life, and it was glorious.

Halfway through the evening, the Duke had a visit from a strange footman. He'd bowed to the King, then continued to speak with his grace. The broad smile on her uncle's face spoke volumes. The conspirators had been apprehended.

The danger was finally over.

After dinner, the gentlemen declined their port and accompanied the ladies to the ballroom, where an orchestra had been set up for those who wished to dance. As Tristan approached her, Roseanna thought she'd never been so happy. With a blinding smile, she accepted his request for a dance. Placing her hand in his, she was just about to speak when there was a sudden commotion at the ballroom entrance. She turned to see what the tumult was, only to see Blackmore's butler standing at the door, brandishing a pistol.

A sense of unreality swamped her as Tristan dropped her hand and began to run. What on earth was Boscastle doing with a gun?

She watched helplessly as the butler slowly raised his hand and pointed the pistol directly at the monarch. Shaking her head in disbelief, she took a step forward, wanting to warn his majesty, but somehow the words were stuck in her throat. She vaguely registered the screaming around her, but every ounce of her was focused on Tristan as he threw himself in front of the King, just as the gun went off.

# Twenty-Three

Boscastle had been the *Revisionist* inside the house.

Seconds after the butler had fired, another shot sounded, and Rosie watched in horror as a bloom of red spread over the front of his chest. Moments later, he collapsed.

Picking up her skirts, she began to run towards the last place she'd seen Tristan. Her heart pounded as she saw his majesty crouch down, focused on someone lying on the floor. '*No, no no,*' she moaned as she unceremoniously shoved aside everyone who would keep her from her love. When there were no more obstructions, she stopped, and the first sob forced itself from her throat. Dropping to her knees, she took his hand. 'Tristan,' she whispered brokenly.

'Sweetheart, you need to give them the space to do what they need to do.' Her father's voice sounded next to her, infinitely gentle, knowing as he tried to pull her away. She shook her head vehemently and fought to free herself from her father's grip. Then she looked up and spied Malcolm crouching on Tristan's other side.

'Let me save him lass,' he murmured, reaching out to touch her shoulder. 'Then ye can have him back.'

When Tristan finally woke three days later, he stared at the sumptuous canopy above his head in confusion. Where the devil was he?

'Bloody hell, ye gave us a scare, laddie.' His head snapped to the left at the sound of Malcolm's voice, then groaned as the pain in his head intensified with the sudden movement.

'What happened?' he croaked.

'Ye saved the King o' England is what happened Tristan Bernart. I ken yer name is already on the lips of every person wi' a pulse from here tae London.'

Tristan frowned, trying to recall what had happened. The last thing he remembered was taking Rosie's hand… 'Roseanna?' he croaked, feeling a sudden white-hot pain across his chest.

'Careful laddie, yer not out o' the woods yet. She's here. In fact, she's hardly left yer side since you were shot.'

'How long have I been here?' Tristan rasped.

'This is the fourth day.' Malcolm answered. 'An I have tae say, ye fair put a damper on the garden party, laddie.'

A sudden bark came from outside the door. 'She can stay fer no more than half an hour and the only reason I'm leaving ye both alone is because yer in no fit state tae ravish a bloody cabbage.'

Seconds later, Roseanna came into the room with Trixie in her arms. Seeing him awake, she gave a sob, and he held out a weak hand.

'I thought you were dead,' she murmured, gripping his fingers. For some reason she was unable to stop crying.

'How can I die now when, for the first time, I've got something to live for?' he whispered. 'As soon as I'm out of this bed, I'll be speaking with your father.'

Roseanna gave a teary laugh 'If you think I'm going to wait that long, Tristan Bernart, you're sorely mistaken. Indeed, I'm fully expecting a proposal within the next five minutes...'

# Epilogue

'How the bloody hell could I have harboured a traitor in my household for eight years?' Nicholas ground out, running his hand through his hair in frustrated disbelief.

The men had been left to their after-dinner port, and it was only now the last guest had departed that they were finally able to speak freely about the debacle of the last week.

'Blackmore's not the only house that's been targeted,' Jamie answered laconically. 'Since Boscastle's demise, our counterfeit Comte has been singing like a canary, so at the end of the day, I think we can console ourselves that the whole operation was a success.'

'And the King is unlikely to forget your loyalty, Nick.' Adam shrugged before adding, 'and not only that, you've curried favour with both Wellington and Grey. Both sides of the house – surely a feat worth celebrating.'

'Not to mention the fact that you didn't have to actually *hold* the deuced garden party once a key member of your staff had been implicated in the conspiracy.' Anthony's delight was entirely unfeigned.

'Not helping,' Nicholas retorted through gritted teeth.

'Most of the guests couldn't return home quick enough to question their own servants, so I'd definitely describe it as a win,' Roan added with a chuckle.

Nicholas sighed in exasperation at his grinning brothers-in-law. 'May I remind you that Tristan nearly died,' he bit out, thinking they were taking the whole deuced business far too lightly.

'But he didn't, and it's no small thing to be in the King of England's debt.' Max's pragmatic comment made the Duke feel slightly better.

'Well, as that's the very last garden party I won't be holding,' the Duke responded drily, 'I suppose it's nice to finish on a high note.'

His companions laughed out loud, revelling in the fact they'd thwarted a conspiracy that was barely surpassed by the Gunpowder Plot over two hundred years earlier. Only Gabriel looked a little pensive.

'What's troubling you, Gabe?' the Duke asked, noting the Viscount's uncommon silence.

Gabriel sighed before laughing ruefully. 'Aside from the fact that my daughter appears to have been in the centre of the whole smoky business almost from the beginning, the possibility that her involvement might have been connected to our wounded footman is troubling, to say the least.'

Christian frowned. 'What makes you say that?'

'Well, the simple fact that she's been stationed outside his bedchamber ever since is a good indication,' Gabriel responded drily. 'But I think the initial clue might have been in her hysterical reaction to his shooting.'

'You think there's something between them?' Nicholas's surprise was genuine.

'I've been waitin' fer one o' ye tae register what's been right in front o' yer noses,' Malcolm commented with a grin. 'But dinnae run away wi' the idea that the lad's done anything untoward, my lord. Tristan Bernart is decent tae his core. If he has feelings fer yer daughter, ye can rest assured his intentions are honourable. The question is, how dae ye feel about a French son-in-law?'

~

In retrospect, the last few days had been like one of those merry go rounds Rosie had ridden whilst staying with Henrietta in Torquay.

Although Tristan had obliged her with a suitably heartfelt proposal, Roseanna knew it didn't really mean anything if her parents refused to accept his suit. Honourable he might be, but he was hardly of noble birth, and no matter how it was prettied up, Rosie well knew that her parents idea of a good match did not an include an ex-convict.

During their stolen moments together provided by Malcolm's hitherto unrevealed romantic side, Tristan had freely divulged the entirety of his background – what he remembered of it anyway. At no point had he tried to sanitise it – in fact, Rosie suspected he deliberately told her the warts and all of it in a deliberate ploy to put her off.

In short, he was an orphan without the remotest idea of his parents' identity, who'd been imprisoned in the most horrific circumstances after being caught stealing an apple. He couldn't remember how long he'd been there before Etienne Babin and the real Comte d'Ansouis had unexpectedly been thrown into the same cell. Their escape especially was truly the stuff of fiction and Rosie found herself engrossed as Tristan described how Roan had taken him on as a cabin boy, eventually seeing to his education. 'I doubt I'd be here now if it hadn't been for him,' he'd finished candidly.

While Rosie couldn't even begin to imagine the awfulness of his early years, if Tristan's intention had indeed been to put her off, he failed woefully, and furthermore, the day before he was finally allowed out of bed, Rosie finally decided that she was going to put an end to any prevaricating on his part. Being honourable was all very well and good, but she very much feared his noble-mindedness might lead him to the ridiculous conclusion that he wasn't good enough for her.

She hadn't yet spoken to her parents – at Tristan's request, since he'd told her unequivocally that he wished to stand before her father on his own two feet. She had, however, finally confided in her sister.

Francesca's initial reaction had been one of baffled anger. She truly couldn't understand why her twin had not shared everything with her like always. For the first time, the two girls were no longer in complete harmony, and it was a difficult change for both of them to come to terms with. Of course, eventually, after ringing a fine peal over her sister's head, Frankie had insisted on knowing every last detail. Regrettably, Rosie's catalogue of scandal was miserably short.

A situation she was determined to rectify at the earliest opportunity. Indeed, Roseanna surprised herself with her resolve. In fairness she'd never been on a mission to be ravished before and was entirely unsure how to go about it, especially after Malcolm put a stop to their illicit tête-à-têtes the very moment he believed his patient's capability had moved beyond that of a green vegetable.

And then, of course, there was the added pressure that they would only be at Blackmore for a few more days...

∽

'What will you do if Papa refuses his suit?' Francesca's question took Roseanna completely by surprise. In truth, she'd been entirely wrapped up in the awful possibility that Tristan might get cold feet and had not allowed herself to dwell on the fact that her father might actually refuse to give his permission.

'I mean, I know Papa dotes on both of us,' her twin continued, 'but I cannot imagine him being overly enthusiastic at the thought of you marrying a Frenchman of unknown descent.'

The two girls were walking along the side of the lake. Behind them the sounds of the final family picnic faded into the background. The following day would see the various members begin to go their separate ways and despite the fact that this particular family gathering had not quite been the light-hearted affair everyone had expected, there was an air of sadness hanging over their last alfresco lunch all together.

Her sister's words were blunt, but Rosie knew she meant well - and at the end of the day, Frankie was only speaking the truth. Unfortunately, her comments simply added to Roseanna's growing anxiety.

It had been three days since she'd had been banished from Tristan's bedchamber. She knew he'd been allowed out of bed, and Malcolm assured her he was getting stronger every day, but despite that, he had not sought her out and, more importantly, he had not yet requested an audience with her father.

'Do you think he will?' Francesca clearly registered the fear in her twin's voice and relented slightly. 'Truly? No, I don't, but I think you should at least speak with Mama, otherwise you risk Papa having an apoplexy from shock.' She gave a rueful chuckle, linking their arms. 'Your habit of keeping everything bottled up inside, sister dearest, is not one of your more endearing traits.'

Rosie sighed and nodded, conscious that her sister spoke the truth. 'I had thought to solve the problem by getting Tristan to ravish me,' she admitted in the spirit of sharing. Francesca stopped dead and favoured her with an incredulous look.

'Please tell me he refused,' she breathed, fighting an uncommon urge to strangle her idiot sister.

'Oh, I didn't tell him,' Rosie retorted. 'I'm not that beef-witted.'

'Beef-witted is not the word I'd have used,' Frankie muttered. 'You haven't done anything foolish, have you? I mean, I know Malcolm imprudently allowed you a little time together, but you haven't done anything more than...' She stumbled to a halt, appalled at the direction her thoughts were taking.

Rosie shook her head. 'Just that one kiss, though I confess it gave me all manner of strange feelings.'

'Did it?' Francesca promptly forgot about keeping her sister on the straight and narrow as she listened to Rosie describe the unexpected sensations Tristan's kiss had provoked.

'If I could just get him to do it again,' Roseanna finished, 'I'm certain Papa would all but march me down the aisle.'

Francesca shook her head at her sister's twisted logic. 'You'd be ruined,' she scoffed.

'Well, according to Grandpapa, Mama and all of her sisters tied their garters in public at least once. I mean…' It was Roseanna's turn to stumble to a halt as she suddenly spied the subject of their discussion walking slowly towards them, seemingly conjured out of thin air.

'Please don't even *think* of trying to get the poor man to ravish you in full view of the entire family,' Francesca warned her. Then as he got closer, she muttered, 'I'm not entirely sure he'd survive the attempt in any case.'

When he finally reached them, Francesca stepped forward with a broad smile and dipped into a curtsy. 'It's good to see you up and about again, Mr Bernart.' A quick sideways glance towards her sister revealed that Roseanna hadn't yet moved, and Frankie's smile slipped a little. At this rate, they'd be here all day.

'How are you feeling, Sir?' she added, tempted to give her sister a swift kick.

Tristan bent his head. 'I'm much improved, thank you my lady. I came to speak with your sister. Would you do us the courtesy of playing chaperone?' Francesca gave a relieved sigh. *Thank goodness*. He at least had no intention of doing any impromptu ravishing.

Another glance towards Rosie showed her sister coming to life at last. With a cordial smile, Francesca inclined her head and turned to stare determinedly out over the lake.

'How are you feeling?' Rosie's voice came out as little more than a squeak and her face flamed.

'I am much better now that I've seen you,' Tristan murmured, stepping closer. For a second, Rosie simply stared up at him, drinking in his silver gaze. She couldn't think of anything remotely witty to say. When he spoke again, she didn't immediately register his words, then as she realised what he'd said, her heart began pumping wildly. For a second, she couldn't breathe.

'I've just come from your father.'

His smile was blinding, and abruptly the pressure in her chest eased and she found herself smiling back as he took her hands.

'He knew, Rosie. Don't ask me how. He's given us his blessing, provided I can prove I have the means to take care of you.'

Roseanna blinked. 'Do you have the means?' she asked in a small voice.

Tristan threw back his head and laughed out loud. 'Believe it or not, I'm a man of considerable means,' he chuckled. 'I may not be of noble birth, but since leaving that hellhole, I have indeed prospered.' He paused before adding, 'I like to think Roan has been repaid many times over for taking such a chance on an unknown *sans culotte*.'

'Sans culotte?' Rosie frowned, searching through her knowledge of French.

'Literally *without breeches*,' Tristan supplied. 'The term was used during the revolution to describe the poorest in France.'

'I don't give a tinker's damn about a title,' Roseanna murmured, 'though I cannot help but look forward to actually seeing you *sans culottes*.' She gave a mischievous laugh of her own at Tristan's sudden indrawn breath.

'Have a care, my lady,' he growled. 'I am not so infirm that I'm unable to take you in my arms and kiss you into surrender.'

'Are you permitted to do that now we're officially betrothed?' Rosie quizzed him breathlessly.

In answer, he lifted his hand and gently stroked his thumb across her lips. His starkly handsome countenance stole her breath away, and the expression in his eyes was one of pure longing. Abruptly, she found herself wanting to throw caution to the winds and demand he ravish her anyway.

'May I remind you that while I might not actually be observing your actions, I am certainly not deaf.' Francesca's comment was dry, causing the strange tension to break.

'My apologies, Lady Francesca.' Tristan murmured huskily without taking his eyes off his beloved. God's teeth, when had he ever wanted a woman as much as he longed for this one? Reluctantly, he let his hand drop before he was tempted to pull her into his arms, bullet wound or no.

Rosie found herself swaying towards him, the same unfamiliar sensations making her legs weak.

'So, you do not consider my lack of blue blood to be a disadvantage,' he said between gritted teeth, attempting to get back to their earlier levity whilst desperately trying to ignore the way her gaze clung to his.

Realising what he was trying to do, Rosie took a deep breath. Zounds, she was turning into a wanton. Truly, the wedding had better be soon.

'A title is nothing but an accident of birth,' she finally managed. 'You have achieved so much more - and against odds that would have broken a lesser man. I'm honoured to become your wife.' She caught the fleeting look of relief in his eyes and felt a sudden fierce joy. How the devil had she managed to catch such an amazing man? She wanted to shout her delight to the world – a completely unfamiliar notion to the Roseanna of old.

Instead, she found herself smiling broadly. 'Who's to say that you're not of noble birth?' she quipped, her happiness bubbling over. 'As you say, you've no idea who your parents were.'

'You might just turn out to be French Royalty...'

## THE END

**The story will continue in Henrietta: Book Four of The Shackleford Legacies to be released on 20th December 2025.**

# Keeping in Touch

Thank you so much for reading *Roseanna,* I really hope you enjoyed it. For any of you who'd like to connect, I'd really love to hear from you. Feel free to contact me via my facebook page:
https://www.facebook.com/beverleywattsromanticcomedyauthor
or my website:
http://www.beverleywatts.com

If you'd like me to let you know as soon as Henrietta is available, and receive a FREE short story introducing The Shackleford Sisters, copy and paste the link below into your browser to sign up to my newsletter and I'll keep you updated about that and all my latest releases.

https://motivated-teacher-3299.kit.com/143a008c18

And lastly, if you're enjoying the Shackleford world and don't want to wait until Henrietta is released, you might be interested to know that I have a series of romantic comedies set in beautiful South Devon, featuring the Great, Great, Great, Great, Great Grandson of the Reverend. In this series he's an eccentric, retired Admiral who, like the Reverend would be in if he fell in...

The series is titled The Shackleford Diaries and in Book One: Claiming Victory, the Admiral is determined to marry off his only daughter, Victory. Keep reading for a sneak peek of Claiming Victory…

# Claiming Victory

At thirty-two, Victory Shackleford is arguably overweight, undeniably frumpish and the love of her life is a dog. She still lives at home with her father – an eccentric, retired Admiral who she considers reckless, irresponsible, and totally incapable of looking after himself. Her father on the other hand thinks Victory is a miserable wet blanket with no imagination or sense of adventure, and what's more he's determined to find her a partner who will take her off his hands.

Unfortunately, there's no one in the picturesque yachting town of Dartmouth that Tory is remotely interested in, despite her father's best efforts. But all that is about to change when she discovers that her madcap parent has rented out their house as a location shoot for the biggest Hollywood blockbuster of the year. As cast and crew descend, Tory's humdrum, orderly existence is turned completely upside down, especially as the lead actor has just been voted the sexiest man on the planet...

*Claiming Victory* is a delightful and witty tale that will have you laughing out loud and rooting for Tory every step of the way. With its quirky characters, laugh-out-loud moments, and unexpected romance, this book is the perfect escape into a world of comedic mayhem. So grab a copy, *sit back, and get ready for a hilarious journey that will leave you smiling from ear to ear!*

# Chapter One

Retired Admiral, Charles Shackleford, entered the dimly lit interior of his favourite watering hole. Once inside, he waited a second for his eyes to adjust, and glanced around to check that his ageing springer spaniel was already seated beside his stool at the bar. Pickles had disappeared into the undergrowth half a mile back, as they walked along the wooded trail high above the picturesque River Dart. The scent of some poor unfortunate rabbit had caught his still youthful nose. The Admiral was not unduly worried; this was a regular occurrence, and Pickles knew his way to the Ship Inn better than his master.

Satisfied that all was as it should be for a Friday lunchtime, Admiral Shackleford waved to the other regulars and made his way to his customary seat at the bar where his long standing, and long-suffering friend, Jimmy Noon, was already halfway down his first pint.

'You're a bit late today, Sir,' observed Jimmy, after saluting his former commanding officer smartly.

Charles Shackleford grunted as he heaved his ample bottom onto the bar stool. 'Got bloody waylaid by that bossy daughter of mine.' He sighed dramatically before taking a long draft of his pint of real ale,

CHAPTER ONE

which was ready and waiting for him. 'Damn bee in her bonnet since she found out about my relationship with Mabel Pomfrey. Of course, I told her to mind her own bloody business, but it has to be said that the cat's out of the bag, and no mistake.'

He stared gloomily down into his pint. 'She said it cast aspersions on her poor mother's memory. But what she doesn't understand Jimmy, is that I'm still a man in my prime. I've got needs. I mean look at me – why can't she see that I'm still a fine figure of a man, and any woman would be more than happy to shack up with me.'

Abruptly, the Admiral turned towards his friend, so the light shone directly onto his face and leaned forward. 'Come on then man, tell me you agree.'

Jimmy took a deep breath as he dubiously regarded the watery eyes, thread veined cheeks, and larger than average nose no more than six inches in front of him.

However, before he could come up with a suitably acceptable reply that wouldn't result in him standing to attention for the next four hours in front of the Admiral's dishwasher, the Admiral turned away, either indicating it was purely a rhetorical question, or he genuinely couldn't comprehend that anyone could possibly regard him as less than a prime catch.

Jimmy sighed with relief. He really hadn't got time this afternoon to do dishwasher duty as he'd agreed to take his wife shopping. Although to be fair, a four-hour stint in front of an electrical appliance at the Admiral's house, with Tory sneaking him tea and biscuits, was actually preferable to four hours trailing after his wife in Marks and Spencer's. He didn't think his wife would see it that way though. Emily Noon had enough trouble understanding her husband's tolerance towards 'that dinosaur's' eccentricities as it was.

Of course, Emily wasn't aware that only the quick thinking of the dinosaur in question had, early on in their naval career, saved her husband from a potentially horrible fate involving a Thai prostitute who'd actually turned out to be a man...

CHAPTER ONE

As far as Jimmy was concerned, Admiral Shackleford was his commanding officer, and always would be, and if that involved such idiosyncrasies as presenting himself in front of a dishwasher with headphones on, saluting and saying, 'Dishwasher manned and ready, Sir.' Then four hours later, saluting again while saying, 'Dishwasher secured,' so be it.

It was a small price to pay... He leaned towards his morose friend and patted him on the back, showing a little manly support (acceptable, even from subordinates), while murmuring, 'Don't worry about it too much, Sir. Tory's a sensible girl. She'll come round eventually – you know she wants you to be happy.' The Admiral's only response was an inelegant snort, so Jimmy ceased his patting, and went back to his pint.

Both men gazed into their drinks for a few minutes, as if all the answers would be found in the amber depths.

'What she needs is a man.' Jimmy's abrupt observation drew another rude snort, this one even louder.

'Who do you suggest? She's not interested in anyone. Says there's no one in Dartmouth she'd give house room to, and believe me, I've tried. When she's not giving me grief, she spends all her time in that bloody gallery with all those airy-fairy types. Can't imagine any one of them climbing her rigging. Not one set of balls between 'em.' Jimmy chuckled at the Admiral's description of Tory's testosterone-challenged male friends.

'She's not ugly, though,' Charles Shackleford mused, still staring into his drink. 'She might have an arse the size of an aircraft carrier, but she's got her mother's top half which balances it out nicely.'

'Aye, she's built a bit broad across the beam,' Jimmy agreed nodding his head.

'And then there's this bloody film crew. I haven't told her yet.' Jimmy frowned at the abrupt change of subject and shot a puzzled glance over to the Admiral.

'Film crew? What film crew?'

CHAPTER ONE

Charles Shackleford looked back irritably. 'Come on, Jimmy, get a grip. I'm talking about that group of Nancies coming to film at the house next month. I must have mentioned it.'

Jimmy simply shook his head in bewilderment.

Frowning at his friend's obtuseness, the Admiral went on, 'You know, what's that bloody film they're making at the moment – big blockbuster everyone's talking about?'

'What, you mean The Bridegroom?'

'That's the one. Seems like they were looking for a large house overlooking the River Dart. Think they were hoping for Greenway, you know, Agatha Christie's place, but then they spied the Admiralty and said it was spot on. Paying me a packet they are. Coming next week.'

Jimmy stared at his former commanding officer with something approaching pity. 'And you've arranged all this without telling Tory?'

'None of her bloody business,' the Admiral blustered, banging his now empty pint glass on the bar, and waving at the barmaid for a refill. 'She's out most of the time anyway.'

Jimmy shook his head in disbelief. 'When are you going to tell her?'

'Was going to do it this morning, but then this business with Mabel came up, so I scarpered. Last I saw, she was taking that bloody little mongrel of hers out for a walk. Hoping she'll walk off her temper.' His tone indicated he considered there was more likelihood of hell freezing over.

'Is Noah Westbrook coming?' said Jimmy, suddenly sensing a bit of gossip he could pass on to Emily.

'Noah who?' was the Admiral's bewildered response.

'Noah Westbrook. Come on, Sir, you must know him. He's the most famous actor in the world. Women go completely gaga over him. If nothing else, that should make Tory happy.'

# CHAPTER ONE

The Admiral stared at him thoughtfully. 'What's he look like, this Noah West—chappy?'

The barmaid, who had been unashamedly listening to the whole conversation, couldn't contain herself any longer, and thrusting a glossy magazine under the Admiral's nose, said breathlessly, 'Like this. He looks like this.'

The full-colour photograph was that of a naked man lounging on a sofa, with only a towel protecting his modesty, together with the caption "Noah Westbrook, officially voted the sexiest man on the planet."

Admiral Charles Shackleford stared pensively down at the picture in front of him. 'So, this Noah chap – he's in this film, is he?'

'He's got the lead role.' The bar maid actually twittered, causing the Admiral to look up in irritation – bloody woman must be fifty if she was a day. Shooting her a withering look, he went back to the magazine and read the beginning of the article inside.

> *"Noah Westbrook is to be filming in the Southwest of England over the next month, causing a sudden flurry of bookings to hotels and guest houses in the South Devon area."*

The Admiral continued to stare at the photo, the germination of an idea tiptoeing around the edges of his brain. Glancing up, he discovered he was the subject of scrutiny from not just the barmaid, but now the whole pub was waiting with bated breath to hear what he was going to say next.

The Admiral's eyes narrowed as the beginnings of a plan slowly began taking shape, but he needed to keep it under wraps. Looking around at his rapt audience, he feigned nonchalance. 'Don't think Noah Westbrook was mentioned at all in the correspondence. Think he must be filming somewhere else.'

Then, without saying anything further, he downed the rest of his drink and climbed laboriously off his stool.

CHAPTER ONE

'Coming, Jimmy, Pickles?' His tone was deceptively casual which fooled Jimmy not at all, and, sensing something momentous afoot, the smaller man swiftly finished his pint. In his haste to follow the Admiral out of the door, he only narrowly avoided falling over Pickles who, completely unappreciative of the need for urgency, was sitting in the middle of the floor, scratching unconcernedly behind his ear.

Once outside, the Admiral didn't bother waiting for his dog, secure in the knowledge that someone would let the elderly spaniel out before he got too far down the road. Instead, he took hold of Jimmy's arm, and dragged him out of earshot – just in case anyone was listening.

In complete contrast to his mood on arrival, Charles Shackleford was now grinning from ear to ear. 'That's it. I've finally got a plan,' he hissed to his bewildered friend. 'I'm going to get her married off.'

'Who to?' asked Jimmy confused.

'Don't be so bloody slow, Jimmy. To him of course. The actor chappy, Noah Westbrook. According to that magazine, women everywhere fall over themselves for him. Even Victory won't be able to resist him.'

Jimmy opened his mouth, but nothing came out. He stared in complete disbelief as the Admiral went on. 'Then she'll move out, and Mabel can move in. Simple.'

Pickles came ambling up as Jimmy finally found his voice. 'So, let me get this straight, Sir. Your plan is to somehow get Noah Westbrook, the most famous actor on the entire planet to fall in love with your daughter, Victory, who we both love dearly, but - and please don't take offence, Sir - who you yourself admit is built generously across the aft, and whose face is unlikely to launch the Dartmouth ferry, let alone a thousand ships.'

The Admiral frowned. 'Well admittedly, I've not worked out the finer details, but that's about the sum of it. What do you think...?'

*Claiming Victory - Book One of the Shackleford Diaries* is available from Amazon

CHAPTER ONE

Turn the page for a complete list of my books on Amazon…

# Also by Beverley Watts on Amazon

### The Shackleford Sisters

Book 1 - Grace

Book 2 - Temperance

Book 3 - Faith

Book 4 - Hope

Book 5 - Patience

Book 6 - Charity

Book 7 - Chastity

Book 8 - Prudence

Book 9 - Anthony

### The Shackleford Legacies

Book 1 - Jennifer

Book 2 - Mercedes

Book 3 - Roseanna

Book 4 - Henrietta will be released on 20th December 2025

### Shackleford and Daughters

Book 1 - Alexandra will be released on 12th June 2025

### The Shackleford Diaries:

Book 1 - Claiming Victory

Book 2 - Sweet Victory

Book 3 - All For Victory

Book 4 - Chasing Victory

Book 5 - Lasting Victory

Book 6 - A Shackleford Victory

Book 7 - Final Victory

**The Admiral Shackleford Mysteries**

Book 1 - A Murderous Valentine

Book 2 - A Murderous Marriage

Book 3 - A Murderous Season

**Standalone Titles**

An Officer and a Gentleman Wanted

# About the Author

**Beverley Watts**

Beverley spent 8 years teaching English as a Foreign Language to International Military Students in Britannia Royal Naval College, the Royal Navy's premier officer training establishment in the UK. She says that in the whole 8 years there was never a dull moment and many of her wonderful experiences at the College were not only memorable but were most definitely 'the stuff of fiction.' Her debut novel An Officer And A Gentleman Wanted is very loosely based on her adventures at the College.

Beverley particularly enjoys writing books that make people laugh and currently she has three series of Romantic Comedies, both contemporary and historical, as well as a humorous cosy mystery series under her belt.

She lives with her husband in an apartment overlooking the sea on the beautiful English Riviera. Between them they have 3 adult children and two gorgeous grandchildren plus 3 Romanian rescue dogs of indeterminate breed called Florence, Trixie, and Lizzie. Until recently, they also had an adorable 'Chichon" named Dotty who was the inspiration for Dotty in The Shackleford Diaries.

You can find out more about Beverley's books at www.beverley-watts.com

Printed in Great Britain
by Amazon